ANNA'S SECRET

ANNA'S SECRET

Margaret A. Westlie

Selkirk Stories
Meadowbank, Prince Edward Island, Canada

Copyright © 2014 Margaret Westlie
All rights reserved.
ISBN-13: 978-0-9936040-4-1

Cover art and design by Anne Gallant
www.annegallantart.ca

Printed by CreateSpace, an Amazon.com Company

Chapter 1

Anna lay as if asleep, her head turned slightly to the side, her auburn hair still neat in its habitual bun. Flies buzzed around her face, landing now on her chin, then on her right ear, drawn by the smell of blood congealing beneath her head. The summer sun burned down on her freckled skin, which was now unguarded by the hat she had always worn. The axe lay nearby.

The boy, Neil, whistled as he strode across the stubbled field, his bare feet silent on the red clay path, his fishing pole balanced across his right shoulder. His melody stopped when he saw Anna lying in the middle of the field.

'Tis a strange place to take a nap, he thought.

A fly landed on her cheek.

She's awful still, he thought. He looked at her more closely. "Mrs. Gillis?" He leaned over and reached out his hand, then drew back without touching her. "Mrs. Gillis?" He spoke more loudly.

Anna did not move. A fly buzzed and crawled over her hair and disappeared behind her head. A few more joined the feast.

"Mrs. Gillis!" Neil shouted. He reached out his hand again and shook her by the arm. He felt the dank cold of her deadness through her dress, and he pulled his hand away from her as if she had burned him instead.

She's dead, he thought. He leaned back on his haunches staring at her. "She's dead!" He repeated it aloud to make it seem more real. He jumped to his feet and began to run, leaving his fishing pole beside the still form that had been Anna Gillis.

"Someone's gone to great pains to leave her comfortable." Angus stared down at Anna. He was a church elder, and because of his wisdom, the unspoken head of the community. The ten minutes since Neil had arrived with his news had seemed an hour.

"Aye, they have indeed." Duncan regarded the neatness of Anna's grey drugget dress arranged modestly around her ankles, her folded hands lying across her abdomen. "It's more than she deserved."

"Hush now, Duncan, it's bad luck to speak ill of the dead."

"Yes, Duncan, she might come back and haunt you," said Hector, his pale blue eyes quite serious.

"Och, Hector, you're always thinking of ghosts." Angus shook his grey head. "The poor thing probably has more to do than come back and haunt the likes of you."

"She's likely dancing in the hot place wishing for a bigger fan," said Duncan.

A giggle erupted from Neil who had been hovering at the periphery of the small group of men. Angus looked hard at Duncan. "No more of that talk now, in front of children." He squatted down beside Anna. "Is this the way you found her, Neil?"

"Yes, sir."

"You didn't touch her?"

"No, sir, only to shake her arm to see if she had just

fallen asleep. She was stiff with the cold."

Angus regarded Anna for another moment. "Help me turn her over, then."

The three men knelt and turned her onto her left side. A small swarm of flies rose from their feast of sticky blood left on the pillow of yellow straw that had supported her head.

"It must have been someone who cared about her to take such trouble with her remains," said Hector.

"Aye, it's as if she was being put to bed," agreed Angus.

"One more time," said Duncan.

"Who's going to tell Ian?" asked Hector.

"I will," said Angus. "He's my own cousin and we've known each other since we were schoolboys."

"But we're his cousins, too," said Duncan.

"Nevertheless, I will tell him. You two will follow with Anna's remains."

"We need something to carry her on," said Hector.

"There's the door to Murdoch's house that's fallen in," said Neil.

"Run, then, and be quick about it. Go with him, Hector, he'll not be able to carry it by himself."

Hector and Neil set out across the field where they

had worked side by side with Ian only a few days before. The oats had been thick that summer and the straw had been plentiful, its shadowy roots home to field mice and grass snakes and crickets. Murdoch's house had long stood vacant, its windows broken and its door fallen off its leather hinges. The roof had blown off in a winter gale three years ago and now the whole structure sat at a crazy angle not quite ready to fall into its cellar.

"You're lighter than I am," said Hector. "Go in and get the other end of the door, but mind where you step, it's none of it very stable."

The floor creaked and moved even under Neil's slight weight. A few moments of careful manoeuvring freed the door from its bed of fallen rafters. In a few minutes Hector and Neil returned to the others.

Neil watched as Hector, Duncan and Angus loaded Anna's remains onto the grey planks of the door. A smear of blood darkened the wood as they positioned her head for the journey home.

Hector shuddered. "Old Annie said this door would be smeared with the blood of the just."

"Will you stop it, Hector," said Duncan. "When did

she say that?"

"The winter before Murdoch left for the Boston States."

"That's years ago, and Annie's senile."

"Not then she wasn't. She said it as plain as day. I was there and I heard her."

"And what did Murdoch think of all that?"

"There's some say that's the reason he left the Island."

"Och, I don't believe it," said Duncan. "A more level-headed man than Murdoch you'd never find. He'd scoff at such an idea."

"Well, all I know is that she said it," said Hector, "and right after that Murdoch went away."

"Will you two stop it," said Angus. "I'll take the axe and go on ahead to Ian. You bring Anna, and mind you don't drop her." He turned on his heel, shouldered the axe, and trudged away across the stubbled field.

I knew the day Ian married her it wouldn't last, he thought. She was too young. And now she's dead and someone's killed her and I hope it wasn't Ian, although he'd have had plenty of reason, with her going off to see James whenever she wanted to. He trudged on, his feet in their homemade shoes quiet on the red clay path. I'm sorry to be the one to bring him such news as this, but it'll be better coming from me than from Duncan or Hector. They're such clowns. He shook his head. It's hard to believe that my own father's brother fathered them, and two of them at once. He quickened his pace through the woods. Poppa and Uncle Johnny were both so level-headed, and Aunt Isabella was too. Indeed, it's hard to explain.

Angus paused at the top of the rise that overlooked Anna's house. Its setting was framed by the distant blue of the Northumberland Strait. The whitewashed house, trimmed in red, nestled in the hollow, flanked by the two barns and the workshop, also whitewashed. A long row of tall fir trees grew close behind, protecting the little farmhouse and its outbuildings from the vicious winter winds that could sweep across Prince Edward Island burying small houses, such as this, in drifts up to the eaves, and freezing a person to his very marrow. Angus shivered and hastened down the track.

I helped Ian build the big barn, and my father and my grandfather helped his father build this house, he thought. Anna planted those chestnut trees by the front door the day they were married. They've grown tall since then, but they've never produced nuts. A strange thing. He rounded the corner of the house and knocked on the door.

"Are you home, Ian?" He pushed the door open with the toe of his shoe.

"I am." Ian's voice sounded tired and far away.

Angus stepped into the sunlit kitchen, the bloody axe forgotten in his hands. His friend looked ill, weary-faced and worn, his eyes were red-rimmed and blood shot. His thick grey beard was still streaked with black and the hair on his head was grey too, except for the cowlick of black springing up from the front above his right eyebrow. He seemed rumpled and unkempt, and a little wild. He hunched his broad shoulders as if to ward off a blow.

"Where's Donald?" asked Angus.

"Finishing the chores." Ian was standing by the unlit stove, his hands busy shaving kindling off a stick of wood with the kitchen knife. "Have you found her, then?" He stared hard at the axe in Angus' hands.

"We found her. Neil found her. They're bringing her soon." Angus followed Ian's gaze, for the first time realizing that he still held the weapon. He almost dropped it in his haste to conceal it behind his back. "I'm sorry, I forgot to set this down." His ruddy cheeks turned a darker shade of red.

"She's dead, is she?" Ian stopped making kindling and stood waiting for the answer.

"She's been murdered."

Ian stood silently taking in the words. "It was bound to happen," he said at last.

"Now why would you say that?"

Ian looked back at his friend, his blue eyes filled with tears. He blinked hard. "I knew about her from the very first time, and every time after that."

"You didn't…?"

"I suppose that's what they'll all be saying when the word gets around." He sighed. "No, it wasn't I, though I have more reason than anyone. Is that the weapon?"

"It would seem so." Angus drew the axe out from behind his back.

"Whose is it?"

"I don't know. I've never seen it before. I suppose we'll have to notify the constable. This thing's too big for us. Though what good he'll be, I don't know."

Ian stood in silence for some seconds, then said, "I was

just making Donald and me a bite of breakfast. Will you have some?" He turned toward the stove.

"I wouldn't trouble you at a time like this. I should be making you breakfast."

Ian shrugged. "We must go on, and to do that we must eat." He began preparing the meal.

Presently the sound of men's voices drifted in through the open window. "Be careful, Duncan. It'll be a fine thing if we drop her in her own dooryard. It was bad enough that we dropped her once."

"I can't help that I tripped," snapped Duncan. "If you hadn't been going so fast, it wouldn't have happened."

"Well, how often do you hear an owl hooting in the broad light of day, I'd like to know. It's an omen of bad things to come."

"I think bad things have already come. How much worse d'you think it'll get?"

Hector ignored him. "Go knock on the door, Neil, and see if they're ready to receive us."

Ian opened the door just as Neil raised his hand to knock. "Bring her inside." Ian stood aside and held the door.

"Where are we to put her?" asked Hector.

"In her own bed." Ian stood aside to let them pass.

"Where she should have been last night and none of this would have happened," grunted Duncan under his breath, as the door that they carried Anna's body on, stuck in the door jamb of the house.

"We'll have to tip her a little." Hector struggled to release the makeshift stretcher.

"Tip her and have her fall off again," said Duncan. "She'll be that bruised they'll have to put a sign with her name on it at her own funeral, so the neighbours know who she is."

"Will you be quiet!" said Hector through gritted teeth. He gave a vigorous tug at his end of the door. "Have some respect. If not for Anna, then for Ian." The door jamb released its hold on the door, and Hector staggered backward, while Duncan lurched forward, each trying to maintain a grip on their heavy burden. They succeeded, and in a few minutes of careful tipping and sliding, Anna was arranged neatly on her marriage bed.

"She always was a fine figure of a woman," gasped Hector as he sat by the bedside for a moment catching his breath. "I fancied her myself when we were young."

"Hush, Hector," said Duncan. "The next thing you know you'll be lusting after a dead woman and her already married. C'mon now, and help me get this door back outside, and we'll offer our condolences to Ian."

By the time they had wrestled the door outside and returned to the kitchen, Donald had joined his father there.

Donald's almost as tall as his father, thought Angus, though that's not saying much. Ian's not tall. In a few years he'll be bigger than him. Donald's dark like Ian, too, kind of ruddy in his face, although there's a look of Anna about his eyes.

"It shouldn't be too hard to find out who did this terrible thing," said Angus. "If we find the owner of the axe, I expect we'll have our man."

"Aye, that's so," said Duncan and Hector together.

"D'you know whose axe it is, Ian?" asked Hector.

The twins' pale bright eyes watched Ian's face.

"No, I've never seen it before. It's got an unusual handle and I would have remembered it."

"Well, I'll get this gruesome thing out of your kitchen, and send my Mary over to help you," said Angus. "We'll get to the bottom of this, right enough." He turned to go. "I'll send Minister MacDonald to you on my way by."

Paddy, the constable, arrived at noon the following day. His shoulders and his moustache drooped, and the burden of his thin form seemed almost too much for him to bear. Angus watched his plodding progress up the hill. His respect in the community was minimal and his services were seldom sought.

"It's good to see you again, Paddy." Angus made a pretence at courtesy. "You got here in good time."

"I started as soon as I got your message," said Paddy. "It's a long walk from Vernon River, and I have to get back for chores. My wife's expecting any day now and can't lift as well as she used to."

"Another one. Well, now," said Angus. "How many does that make?"

"Too many." Paddy's rounded shoulders drooped even farther with the expectation of further parental duties. "It's hard to feed the ones we've got." He sighed. "I hear you've had a murder."

"Aye, that we have." Angus nodded. "It was Anna Gillis.

She was found yesterday morning in a field, with her head bashed in with an axe."

"Let me be the judge of that," droned Paddy.

"The axe was lying right beside her, man, there's not much to judge about that."

"Nevertheless, I am the law."

Angus shrugged. "Whatever you say."

"Where is she?"

"At home, lying on her bed until they can get a casket made for her."

"You moved her?"

"We couldn't leave her lying there all night. It was bad enough that she was there all the previous night and no one knew about her, with the flies feasting on her blood. The next thing you know she'd have been eaten by the ravens."

"No, I suppose not." Paddy blinked his pale grey eyes at the gruesome possibility. "It's a shame though, to have disturbed the scene of the crime."

"There's not much scene to it. There was just her on a pillow of straw and the axe lying beside her."

"You'll have to show it to me anyway."

"It's in Ian's big hill field. They had just harvested the

oats a few days ago, and she was lying beside the path as neatly placed as if she'd just lain down to have a nap." Angus led the way down the track toward Ian's.

The morning was bright with sunshine. Wrens warbled and trilled. The distinctive chick-a-dee-dee-dee of black-capped chickadees sounded nearby and was answered from across the meadow. A salt breeze from the Gulf of St. Lawrence sifted through the branches of the trees, rustling the leaves of birches, oaks and maples. The air was warm with the smell of pine and spruce and the sea, mixed with the sweet odour of ferns crushed underfoot as they walked. Somewhere nearby a single locust sawed loudly. Ahead of them a dark blue dragon fly hovered and dipped in the sunlight. Together they climbed the hill and crossed the field.

"It was here that she was." Angus stopped on the path and pointed to the pillow of straw stained dark with Anna's blood.

"And the axe was beside her?"

"Just there." Angus pointed to a spot slightly to the left of the pillow.

Paddy bent over and examined the site more closely,

his narrow rump pointing heavenwards. "It's too bad that you had to move her and the axe, too."

"Humph!" said Angus, "I told you already, we couldn't leave her here in the field while we waited for you to show your face. It took you long enough as it was."

Paddy glanced up. "I came as fast as I could. She wasn't going anywhere in a hurry was she?"

"According to you she was," said Angus. "Have you looked enough yet? I don't like being here. It makes me uneasy."

Paddy straightened up. "I guess so. There's not much to see anymore, is there? I don't suppose you have any idea who did it?"

"That's what I called you for."

"What was she doing here at that time of night anyway?"

"She was visiting a neighbour." Angus turned toward the path. "We think she was on her way home."

Paddy followed him, his homely face made homelier by the scowl of his thoughts. "Did she get along with everyone?"

"As well as anyone."

"What about her husband?"

"Ian? What about him?"

"Did she get along with him?"

"As far as anyone knew."

"I'd like to talk to him."

"He'll have nothing to tell you. He and his son, Donald, were together all evening."

Paddy sighed. "What about the people she was visiting?"

"Person. No one's seen him, and he's not at home."

Suddenly the pieces fell together for Paddy. "Oh, that Anna. Rumour has it that she was playing on the side with an old boyfriend." His homely features lighted into the beginning of a smile, then fell back upon themselves with the effort required.

"It was only a rumour. There was nothing in it." Angus quickened his step. "There's Ian's house. I have to be going. He can direct you wherever you want to go next." He turned on his heel and strode back the way he'd come.

Paddy's investigation was over in a day. In that brief time of sunshine and birdsong he managed to alienate everyone in the community, and they closed ranks against him.

"He's a daft Irishman," said Duncan. "What he knows about investigating isn't worth knowing."

"He only took the job for the money," said Hector. "He

said so once. He's had no training."

"With all those children he needs the money. That's about all he's good for, that and complaining."

Paddy's report described Anna's death as an accident. His superiors in Charlottetown shook their heads, considered starting another investigation, then filed his report under Accidents.

In the curve of the dark spruce woods gleamed the whiteness of St. John's church surrounded by its tidy graveyard. The neatness was marred only by the gape of the freshly dug grave that was to be Anna's final resting place. The church was filled with neighbours and relatives; in fact, most of the neighbours were relatives in varying degrees. Anna lay in her plain wooden casket at the front of the church, all evidence of her injury washed away, her face turned slightly toward the congregation to hide the dent behind her right ear.

Ian sat in the mourners' bench and stared stonily ahead, his gaze barely taking in his wife's body just a few feet in front of him. His expression was hidden by the thickness of his beard which for once had been brushed into smoothness and trimmed neatly around the edges. His eyes were downcast. His broad shoulders stretched at the seams of his wedding suit, too small for him now after fourteen years of heavy toil on his little farm. A black top hat, borrowed from John the Store, perched incongruously on his knees. Donald sat beside him in equal stillness, emulating the manners of his father, his face strained to whiteness in his effort not to cry.

The church was silent except for the rustle of breathing, and the occasional stifled cough. There were few tears for Anna. From the far corner in the back pew a child's shrill voice whined, "But I want to see." It was instantly hushed and the silence came again.

Presently Minister MacDonald entered and climbed to the pulpit. He had been sent by the church in Scotland to minister to these children of the Highlands thirty years ago. By now it seemed as if he were one of their own. He stood for a moment surveying his flock, his black suit giving him the air of a great raven roosting over the congregation. "Let us pray," he intoned in Gaelic. The congregation rose as one body to pray and afterwards reseated themselves, and the long service began.

Mr. MacDonald adjusted his glasses on the end of his nose and cleared his throat. "Proverbs 31:10." He cleared his throat again.

"Who can find a virtuous woman, for her price is far above rubies?" In the very back of the church someone snorted. Mr. MacDonald glared out into the dimness.

"The heart of her husband doth safely trust in her so that he shall have no need of spoil," he continued. "She will do him good and not evil all the days of her life.

"Anna Gillis' memory will live on in our hearts. You have all known her since she was a child."

"Some better than others," said Duncan under his breath.

Hector nudged him and shook his head.

"She has been a faithful communicant with this congregation all her life. Her presence here will be sorely missed. I doubt that she has missed a Sabbath in church except at the birth of her son, and that of her daughter beside whom she will lie this day. Her help in the work of this congregation was immeasurable." He paused to draw breath.

"Aye, that's as may be," muttered Duncan again, "but

it's what she did after church that got her in this fix."

"Will you be quiet," whispered Hector. "Have some respect for Ian, at least."

Duncan looked ashamed and subsided into silence.

"We can look to Anna's life as an example, even as we look to the ancient Christians for that example. Both their sins and their acts of faith are recorded for our benefit that we should learn to avoid their errings, to guard against sin, to imitate their virtues, and to walk in piety so as to obtain the blessing promised to godliness. In the same way, Anna's life in all its sin and virtue can lead us to the godly path."

Mr. MacDonald trudged on through his sermon. The congregation grew restive. Somewhere a child whimpered and was hushed by its mother. A man sneezed and blew his nose with a loud trumpet. Few tears were shed for Anna.

"When Israel was camped at Shittim, the people began to commit fornication with the daughters of Moab and to participate in their idolatrous festivals. But this sin cost them dearly, for the plague took twenty-three thousand in one day. Be forewarned! Whoremongers and adulterers God will judge! He will condemn them, though once they were His children. Let us pray.

"Heavenly Father, we offer our prayers of intercession for the soul of Anna Gillis. In your mercy, remember the good she has done for this community. Forgive her the sins she may have committed, and lay them not hard against her. Remember her husband, Ian, and her son, Donald. Be with them in this time of great sorrow. We ask these things in Jesus' name. Amen."

The congregation stirred and rose as one body to file silently past the open casket, each one searching for a sign of the blow that had taken Anna.

The pall bearers closed the lid over Anna's still face and nailed it shut. They shouldered its weight and carried their burden to the gaping red hole in the ground. The day had grown cool and overcast, and the birds were as silent as the people who followed the pallbearers.

Mr. MacDonald waited until everyone had assembled then began the ceremony of committal. "The Lord is my shepherd, I shall not want. He maketh me to lie down in green pastures …"

For once Duncan held his tongue.

"Ashes to ashes, from dust we came, unto dust we shall return." The clumps of earth echoed hollowly off the top of the casket. Ian forgot himself and rubbed the residue of soil on his hands onto his pant leg, leaving a streak of red behind.

"Into Thy hands we commend the spirit of our sister Anna Gillis."

"A fine funeral, Mr. MacDonald," said Angus leaning on his shovel for a moment. "It must have been a difficult sermon to preach."

Mr. MacDonald pursed his lips before replying. "No. In fact it was one of the easier ones I've done."

Angus looked at him in surprise. "It was?"

"Indeed it was. She was as good a woman as I said she was, and perhaps even a little better." He turned on his heel and strode away. Angus stared after him for a moment then returned to the task of filling in the grave.

I wonder where James was? It's strange he would miss her funeral. Him of all people. He whistled a hymn tunelessly under his breath as he worked. He paused to wipe the sweat from his eyes. *Where are Duncan and Hector? It's just like them to disappear when there's work to be done.* He pulled off his coat and rolled up his sleeves. *I'd better not get any mud on this good white shirt or Mary'll be* cross. She says the red mud is just like dye, once it's in, it's the devil's own job to get it out. He chuckled to himself. I'll be wearing pink shirts for awhile if that happens.

Another fifteen minutes of hard work saw the job almost finished just as Hector and Duncan hurried around the end of the church.

"You're almost done," said Duncan.

"He always was a fast worker," said Hector, "and a fine job he's done, too."

"Well, you two showed up at the right time, as usual." Angus scraped the last of the dirt onto the grave mound and patted it down with the back of the shovel.

"We were over at the store. I was all out of tobacco," said Duncan. He chewed rhythmically on a mouthful of the black stuff.

"Gossiping, more than likely." Angus threw down the shovel and wiped his sweating hands on the seat of his trousers.

Duncan looked hurt. "No, just getting the news. I wouldn't call it gossiping."

"So, what is the news?"

"Did you not wonder where James was today?" He spat

a stream of rich tobacco juice into the bushes and waited for Angus' reply.

"The thought had crossed my mind." Angus rolled down his sleeves and picked up his coat.

"He's gone," said Hector. "No one's seen him since the day before yesterday."

"That's strange," said Angus. "Has he taken a trip?"

"No one seems to know," replied Hector. "He's just gone."

"The next thing you know, he'll be turning up dead too," said Duncan.

"And it wouldn't be too good for him, either," said Hector. "It'll teach him to leave married women alone."

"Maybe they're down there sharing the fan right now," said Duncan.

"I doubt that," said Angus, "though I don't know where he'd go. The last time he came back to the Island he said he was here to stay. Maybe he's just gone visiting. He has a brother up in Stanchel. He could be there."

Chapter 2

The setting sun cast a narrow ray of light into the darkening kitchen. A whisper of dust covered every surface, and wood chips had begun an invasion from the wood box. Night shadows concealed the worst of the neglect.

Ian sat in the rocker, cradling the white mug with the cold remains of his suppertime tea in his hands, his stockinged feet propped up on the open oven door. The stove was still warm from supper, and that, combined with the heat of the July day just past, made the air stifling, even with the window open. Donald was out doing chores.

Ian pulled out his crumpled handkerchief and mopped his brow. *I suppose I should go and help him,* he thought. *Work'll be better for the both of us just now.* He rose to carry his mug to the pantry where he added it to the stack of dishes waiting to be washed and put away.

"Ah, Anna, why'd you do such a thing?" He stood for a moment surveying the pantry, foreign to him in its present untidiness. She would never see her home in such a state, he thought, but I cannot do it all. Anna! He turned away.

"Are you home, then, Ian?" Angus' voice sounded from the kitchen door.

"Angus! Come in! It's good of you to come. Have a seat."

Angus came in and took the chair on the other side of the stove, noticing peripherally the slight air of untidiness that had taken over the kitchen in the past week. He could not see the pantry from where he sat. "Where's Donald?"

"Out doing chores. I was just about to join him."

"He's a good lad."

"Aye, he is that, and can work like a man now, and him only thirteen."

"He's big for his age."

"He'll be bigger than me when he's done growing. I only wish that Anna could have lived to see him. He was the apple of her eye, and she set such a store by him."

"And he by her."

"She wanted him to go to college and be a teacher. She'd been saving her money to that end all these years."

"She'd be the one to do it. She must have had quite a nest egg by now."

"I don't know. She never told me, and now she's gone." Ian sat staring at his calloused hands. "Have you any news on the murder weapon?"

"No, but James is gone."

"Gone where?"

"No one knows, unless it's to visit his brother up in Stanchel."

"He'd never visit there. They had a fight years ago and they weren't speaking. I don't think they've seen each other since."

"Perhaps we need to send out enquiries. He may have gone off the Island altogether."

"If he's on the run, he probably has. It'd be the sensible thing to do. But why would he be on the run? What reason would he have to harm Anna?"

"Well, now, Ian, not to say that he did without any proof, but they might have quarrelled. It could have been an act of passion."

"Better an act of passion than cold-blooded murder for my Anna."

Angus sat looking at his friend for a few moments. He cleared his throat, then asked, "Are you sure it wasn't you that did it? You'd have had plenty of reason."

Ian scowled. "How can you say such a thing? She meant my life to me. She gave me a son in my old age. She was kind and gentle, and no matter what she's done, she was a good wife. Besides, I was here all evening with Donald."

"Well, that's a relief to know." Angus rose to his feet. "It's good to see you taking this so well. I'll set those enquiries in motion tomorrow. In the meantime if you need anything, send Donald over with a message."

Several days passed before news came that James had indeed left the Island.

"He was in a terrible hurry," said James' cousin, Roddy, as he sat in Angus' kitchen after supper one evening.

Roddy usually worked in Charlottetown, but once a week his duties called him to Orwell to the Brush Wharf, where he sold tickets for the Atlantic Coast Shipping Company and oversaw the loading of produce bound for

Charlottetown, Halifax, and the Boston States.

"He wanted a ticket as far as his money would take him. I gave him one to Boston. I asked him where he was going and at first he wouldn't tell me. He just said it was a terrible thing, and that he couldn't stay here anymore."

"I see," said Angus. "And what day was this?"

"A week ago, first thing in the morning."

"Well, that would be about right." Angus stroked his beard thoughtfully. "Did he say anything else at all?"

"I quizzed him a little, and he finally said, 'She's dead and it's all my fault.' Then he hurried out of the office and was gone, and I haven't seen him since. He had his fiddle with him, so I guess he's gone for good."

"Hm, I wonder." Angus thought for a moment. "So he's gone to Boston?"

Roddy shrugged. "That's where he bought a ticket for, though he could have gotten off anywhere in between. Who is it that's dead? Since I took that job in Charlottetown I don't hear the news much anymore."

"Anna Gillis was found murdered the other morning. We don't know who did it."

Roddy looked surprised. "And you're suspecting James?"

"I'm considering all possibilities."

"I don't think James could have done such a thing. He was always a dreamer and not very strong. Anna was a big strapping woman. She'd have been able to overpower the likes of James."

"Not in this case. She was struck in the head with an axe."

"I see." Roddy scratched his chin. "But what would be his reason? He loved her. He has done since we were children."

"Well, there you have it. She was a married woman, and he was lusting after her, and she after him. The two of them were in it together."

"That doesn't make sense. If they were both in it together, why would he kill her?"

"Jealous that she was with Ian and he couldn't have her?" suggested Angus.

"More likely it was Ian himself that did it. He was the one being wronged."

"Ian said he was home with Donald all evening and Donald says the same thing."

"The pair of them could be lying."

"I don't think so. Ian blushes when he lies. He always has done. Besides, if you could see him, he's that dejected."

"Well, you know him better than I do." Roddy folded his lips tightly for a moment. "So you think it's more likely that James did it?"

Angus sighed. "I don't know what to think. I've known them all since they were children. I haven't even had the heart to clean her blood off the axe yet."

"You have the axe? Well, why didn't you say so? I'll know James' axe. I cut wood with him last fall, and besides, he always puts his initials on his tools."

"C'mon out then, and I'll show it to you." Angus led the way into the dark dustiness of the woodshed, its floor springy with years of bark and wood chips. "It's there in the corner. I'll just get some water and clean it off."

He returned in a few moments with a bucket of water to find Roddy standing with the axe in his hands looking very sad.

"It's James' axe all right. I'd know it anywhere, even without his signature. He favoured that style of handle because he was always a little short in the arms. He said that it gave him a better swing and he needed all the help he could get, him being so short and slight. He carved the handles himself. No one else could use his axe because the handles were too short."

"Well, let's clean it up and see about this signature."

Angus dipped the axe head in the cold water and scrubbed at it with a rag. Anna's life stained the water a rusty brown. "Now show me where this name is." He handed the axe back to Roddy.

"There, by the head." Roddy's stubby finger pointed to the initials etched into the axe handle.

They both stared at the tiny letters in James' distinctive handwriting. Roddy sighed. "Oh, James, what have you done?"

John's store supplied the need of the community for manufactured goods, and for most of the gossip. The store had been there since the second year of the settlement. John's father had built it and the fathers of all the people who now benefited from it had helped. Its dim interior overflowed with items necessary to the progress of the settlers. There were seeds for planting, tools for harvesting, leather for harness, and luxuries like candy and tobacco.

Horse collars and yokes for oxen hung from the ceiling and household brooms stood by the door. On the shelves behind the counters were bolts of brightly coloured cotton, and boxes of buttons. A cabinet of drawers held papers of pins, spools of thread and other necessities for home sewing. In the shadowy spaces left over there were nail kegs and empty molasses puncheons convenient for sitting on. At the end of the counters stood stained brass spittoons placed at just the right angle for men skilled in the art of chewing tobacco. John could order anything else they needed from Charlottetown.

"He must have been in a jealous rage," said Duncan. "He'd not have had the strength otherwise." He sent a stream of tobacco juice accurately into the spittoon at the end of the counter.

"But why would he be in a jealous rage, I'd like to know?" asked Hector. "He had her even though she was married to Ian." He shifted his weight on the nail keg. "It was more likely Ian who was in a jealous rage, his wife stepping out with another man, and him unable to do a thing about it."

"But Angus, you said that Ian and Donald were together

all evening," interrupted John, deftly cutting tobacco into smaller blocks and wrapping it. "It couldn't have been him."

"He could have sneaked out in the middle of the night and done it," said Lochie's son, Neil, from the shadows. It was he who had found Anna when he was on his way to a day of fishing.

"What're you doing here?" asked Lochie. "You're supposed to be working."

"But he could have," insisted Neil, trying to divert his father's attention.

"Finishing your work's more important than who murdered Anna Gillis, now be off with you," thundered Lochie, his tea-stained moustache bristling with annoyance.

Neil slammed the door behind himself.

"He's right, you know." Alexander, a man of Angus' and Lochie's age, propped his chair on its back legs and puffed comfortably on his pipe. "He could have slipped out without Donald ever knowing he was gone."

"And so could any one of us have done it," said William MacMillan, another community stalwart.

"What would be the motive?" asked Duncan. "You

weren't seeing her on the side too, were you?" He cast a crafty glance in William's direction.

"Certainly not! I'm an elder in the church and a married man besides. What would I be doing out running around with the likes of Anna?"

"Well, I don't think either one of them was doing much running," said Hector. "I don't think they were ever in a position to run."

The men laughed.

William scowled. "I don't think we should be making sport of this. It's a serious matter, never mind that she was Ian's wife."

"She was brought before the elders one time wasn't she?" asked Murdoch. He was also an elder but lived farther out than the others so didn't join them informally as often.

"That was years ago," replied William. "It was before I was asked to serve, so I don't know what it was all about."

"I heard that it was for running around with James when she was engaged to Ian," said Hector. "Her father said that he couldn't do a thing with her. It was right after that that James left for Boston and didn't come back for years."

"It was a good thing, too, and maybe he should have

stayed there," said Duncan. "If he had, then perhaps none of this would have happened."

The others murmured their agreement.

"Angus, you've been looking into it. D'you think it was James who did it?" asked Lochie.

Angus sat on a sack of oats with his arms folded on his chest, one hand stroking his beard. His blue eyes were brightly alert. "Well, it does seem so. After all, it was done with his axe, and he's the one who left without saying a word. He knew she was dead before he ever left, because it was him that told Roddy."

It was now late summer and cold weather was not far off. The smell of autumn was in the air at milking time in the mornings, and here and there the trees were beginning to turn their colours. Soon the Island would be bright with the red of maples and the yellow of birch and a whole range of colours in between.

Talk and speculation flowed freely at Mary's house, as the ladies of the community busily plied their needles to Mary's quilt.

"Such lovely material this is, Mary," said Catherine

Finlayson. A spinster by choice, she had done her duty as eldest daughter when her own mother died in childbirth. "Where'd you get it?"

"From John's. I had him order it especially. I've always wanted a quilt made with it. It's so much finer woven than what I can do here on my own loom. I had a little money put by for it, so I said to myself, 'Mary, you're not getting any younger. If you're going to have a quilt of that stuff, now's the time to do it, before you're too old to enjoy it.' I talked it over with Angus and he put the order in for me."

"Speaking of John's," said Flora Shaw, "my Alexander was there the other day and the men were saying that the axe that killed Anna belonged to James. Can you beat that?"

"I'm surprised it didn't happen sooner," sniffed Eliza MacMillan. "From what William told me, they'd been seeing each other much longer than I'd ever suspected."

"Where've you been all these years?" teased Edith MacRae. "It's common knowledge they've been, shall we say, 'friendly,' for years." Edith, a distant cousin to Old Annie, had the care and keeping of her in her dotage.

"Well, I knew they were like brother and sister when they were children," said Eliza, "but he was away for so long, and she was married to Ian …" Her voice trailed away into silence.

"He should have stayed away," said Catherine Gillis, "but he came back, and there they were, and her no better than she should be, even if she was my own sister-in-law. I don't know how Ian put up with it, these past few years, indeed I don't."

"She was very kind to me after the children were born," said Mattie Matheson, wife of the school teacher, but no one heard her. Mattie's hair was turning grey and her children were soon old enough to go out on their own. Her first child, Helen Margaret, was married and soon to deliver her own first baby.

"There's some said that Donald wasn't Ian's," offered Flora. "I heard that he was actually James'."

"Oh, I don't think so," said Mary, "all you have to do is look at him. He has the look of Ian about him. He's much too tall to have been any relation of James'."

"James was the only slight one in that family," said Eliza. "Donald could have taken after old Malcolm if James' father was his grandfather. He was plenty tall."

"Now, Eliza, we don't know what went on there,"

chided Mary. "Donald looks like Ian, and even more like Ian's father. You never knew him, but he was a fine big man, and Donald has his chin and nose. There's no doubt in my mind but that Donald is Ian's son."

"If you say so, Mary," sniffed Flora. "I wouldn't know from Anna's carrying on."

Mary frowned at Flora. "I say so, Flora. Anna was my friend, and a friend to all of you. She was kind and generous, and I don't want to hear another word about it in my house. I have to go for water, and when I come back I want the topic of conversation to have changed." She turned and picked up the bucket from the shelf. "I'll only be a minute."

"Well, I guess I know where I stand," said Flora when Mary had closed the door.

"You did ask for it," said Eliza. "You know that Anna and Mary were good friends."

"Not that good a friends."

"But they were," said Edith. "Anna was good friends with anyone she chose to be friends with. If she didn't choose to, she could be as distant as that wall over there. I should know, for we had a falling out when we were children and to this day she has only been polite to me, though she often used to come and visit with Annie."

"They were great friends ever since Annie taught her all she knew about herbs and weeds," said Catherine Gillis.

"That's right," said Edith. "When Annie was in her right mind she always used to say that Anna would be a better healer than herself."

"She must have been pretty good then, because Annie wasn't given to sharing the glory," said Catherine.

"She was quite mean with her praises too," said Edith. "She always said that she didn't want anyone to get a swelled head on her account."

"By the way, where is Annie today?" asked Eliza.

"She hasn't been well these last few days, so I asked Lochie's Isabelle to stay with her for the afternoon."

"Is she old enough to be sitting with people already? It only seems like yesterday that she was born."

Edith nodded. "Isabelle's the youngest, but she's a good reliable child, and she only has to make sure that Annie doesn't wander off or get hurt. Sam's around today, anyway."

"Look who I found at the well," said Mary. The door thumped and bounced behind her as she assisted Old Annie into the kitchen. The door opened again as Isabelle entered the room carrying the bucket of water.

"What are you doing here?" demanded Edith. "You were supposed to take care of Annie at home."

Isabelle began to cry. "I-I tried to, but she kept getting away and I was afraid I would hurt her if I hung onto her. She was that determined to go her own way, the only thing I could do was to come with her. I'm so sorry."

"It's all right, Isabelle, you did fine." Edith rose from her chair and went to Annie. "Annie has a mind of her own when she wants. Don't you, Annie?"

Annie nodded vacantly.

Edith helped Annie onto the lounge and tried to cover her with a blanket. "You must be tired, Annie. That was a long walk. Why don't you lie here and have a little rest until it's time to go home."

"No, no." Annie pushed the blanket aside and tried to sit up. "I must see Angus." She swung her legs off the edge of the lounge.

"Annie, Angus is out working. He won't be back until suppertime." Mary sat down on the lounge beside Annie and put an arm around her shoulders. "Why don't you tell me what you want and I'll be sure and tell Angus when he comes in." She brushed back the wisp of hair that had fallen into Annie's faded blue eyes.

Annie peered into Mary's face. "Is that you, Mary?"

"Yes, Annie, it's me."

Annie peered more closely. "Oh, but you've aged so. Where's Angus? I suppose he's old too."

"We're of an age," said Mary. "D'you want me to call him in from the fields?"

"No, no just tell him that I'm going to see Anna soon. She was killed, you know. Killed by one who loves her."

"Angus knows that already, Annie."

"No, oh no, he doesn't. Not like I know it. I told her years ago to do what she should do and not say a word, for it would only cause distress." Annie raised her thin hand and rubbed the back of her head. "It was here that she was struck down, but it's here where she hurts." Annie rubbed her thin chest and yawned. "I'm tired. Let me lie down." She lay back on the pillows of the lounge and was soon asleep.

"Well," said Eliza, "I wonder what that performance was all about."

"Och, it's hard to say with Annie. She wanders so these days," said Edith. "I suppose you'd better tell Angus what she said in case he knows what she's rambling about."

To Ian the days seemed never-ending. Each time he looked at his son he could see Anna in Donald's expression. He could hardly bear to look at him, and as the days passed he grew more silent.

"Poppa, I brought Mr. MacDonald to visit," said Donald one evening.

Ian sat beside the cold stove with Anna's thimble in his large hands turning it over and over. The layer of dust had thickened and now dulled the kitchen's previous bright cleanliness. Wood chips covered the floor by the wood box and were slowly spreading to the rest of the kitchen. The curtains, still hanging neatly in the windows, looked dull and lifeless, as if the starch that had held their shape had departed them. Ian's beard, which had been newly trimmed for Anna's funeral, was now ragged and unkempt. His left shirt sleeve showed an unmended, three-cornered tear. He looked up, then rose to his feet.

"Will you have a seat, Mr. MacDonald." He tried to

smile. "You'll have to excuse the condition of the house, I don't have Anna's touch as a housekeeper."

"I wouldn't expect you to, Ian." Mr. MacDonald took the chair across from Ian. "She was a fine housekeeper."

"She was that," agreed Ian. "She kept her home spotless. I could never say a word against her there."

"There's some say plenty against her elsewhere." Donald sat down by the crumb-laden table.

"Don't you speak about your mother that way," said Ian. "She was a good woman no matter what others may say. Now, there's plenty of work to be done, and I'd be obliged if you'd go and do it."

Donald stared at the floor, but rose obediently and did not slam the door as he went out.

"This has taken him hard too," said Mr. MacDonald.

"It's all this talk about Anna. He hears it from the other lads in school. He always thought the world of her and it's changed him."

"Well, no matter what they say, she was a good woman. It's only ignorance talking."

"Aye, she always was. I remember her as a child, so bright and merry. It was always a puzzle to me how she could be so, with her father like he was."

"I've heard that he was a hard man."

"She married me because of him, you know."

"I remember. She was to have married James until her father stepped in, wasn't she?"

Ian nodded. "She went a little wild after that. She could be very sly and secretive when she wanted to be. She was like her father, Sandy, in that. She used to slip away to spend time with James when Sandy was occupied about the farm. There was little he could do about it. He found out one day and was in a terrible rage over it, but she kept it up anyway. That was the time she was reprimanded by the elders. That was before you came here. Her father turned her over to them. She behaved a little better after that for awhile, but then she started in again. I had just lost Belle. She died in childbirth and the child with her. I was very lonely and forsaken. Sandy asked me if I would marry Anna to save her from disgrace. I had no reason not to, so we got married. She was a very reluctant bride, and so shy. She ran off to James once more the night before the wedding and I went after her and brought her home. I had a few words with James that night, and he left for the Boston States right away, and only returned a few years ago, after his own father died. He's been trying to run the farm there all by himself, but he's no farmer. He should have stayed away."

"It would have saved everyone a great deal of trouble. But perhaps Anna and James had a secret that kept them together all these years."

Ian sat staring at his hands for some minutes without speaking. When he spoke again, a great sadness was in his voice. "Whatever the draw, she was over there as soon as she heard that he'd come back, and there was not a thing I could do about it."

"Well, she won't be going there anymore."

Ian turned his hands over and stared down at their calloused palms as if he hadn't heard. "Many a time I forbade her to go, but it was no use. She'd just stand there and smile and agree with me, and then as soon as my back was turned, she'd be off over there again." Ian leaned his shaggy grey head in his hands. "I'd have stopped her if I could."

"You did the best you could. She made her own choices."

"I was never able to see what the attraction was. The

only thing that I could think of was that it was because I am an old man."

"Och, you're not an old man, Ian. You're just in your prime. A man of maturity. What could she have been thinking of?"

"I'm fifty-six. Old enough to have been her father, and James was her own age."

"A mere lad compared to yourself."

"Hardly that anymore. James and Anna were of an age. He was always full of poetry and stories and philosophy. They say women like that sort of thing. I was never good at it myself."

They talked together until night darkened the kitchen and men's voices were heard in the yard.

"You'll tell your father what you've done, or I will," threatened Angus.

"And I'll help him," scolded Hector.

"You should be ashamed, you young imp," said Duncan, "and your mother not cold in her grave yet."

The three men erupted into the shadowy kitchen, pushing Donald ahead of them.

Ian rose to his feet and went to light the candle.

"What's this? Where've you been?" The candle flared into brightness, lighting the room and Donald's rumpled figure and dirty clothes.

"Out."

"Finishing chores, I don't doubt," said Ian.

"They're done." Donald stared at the floor.

"What have you been up to? Why are these men here?"

Donald shrugged one shoulder and didn't reply.

"Answer me!"

"I was over at James'."

"Look at me when you speak to me! What were you doing over there?"

Donald stared at his father's right ear and did not reply.

Ian looked at Angus. "Why have you brought my son home to me?"

"He was over at James' breaking the glass out of the windows. Duncan and Hector were passing by when they heard it and came and got me. He was just finishing off the last one when I got there."

"We were on our way home from William's and we heard the glass breaking," said Duncan.

"He broke every one of the windows before we could

stop him," said Hector. "I thought it was the *bocans* up to mischief, or I would have gone in with just Duncan."

"Oh, *bocans*, indeed." said Angus. "If evil spirits, such as they, exist at all, I doubt they'd be able to break glass. You were too scared to go alone with just Duncan."

Ian ignored the argument and turned again to Donald. "Is this true?"

Donald stared again at the floor and nodded.

"Look at me, Donald!" Ian roared. "Is this true?"

Donald glared at his father. "It's true."

"Why would you do such a thing?"

Donald stared hard at Ian. "It was he who caused my mother's death."

Chapter 3

Ian sat in the shadowy dimness of the kitchen for some time after his neighbours left.

I felt like doing that myself, not so many years ago, he acknowledged to himself, but I restrained myself. Perhaps I shouldn't have. Maybe I should have confronted the two of them and had it out once and for all. Maybe none of this would have happened.

He thought of Anna and how she had been, her long auburn hair silky against his calloused hands at night. Ah, Anna we should have had a half a dozen, he mourned, then maybe you wouldn't have had time to be running over there. But there was only ever Donald and the little one that you're lying next to. She only lived a few hours, and you changed after that.

Ian rubbed his face. It did not wipe away the pain. We didn't even name her. There's some say that she wasn't mine, that she belonged to James. Maybe so, but Donald's mine, he thought. He's too big to be kin to James. Donald's already broadening into a man. James is a pale ghost compared to him.

The candle sputtered and the flame wavered then grew steady again. Ian got up and blew it out. Waste not, want not, he thought absently, his mind still on Anna. Overhead he heard Donald stir restlessly in his sleep. The restlessness communicated itself to him and he went to stand by the open door and stared out across the moonlit fields. Somewhere a dog barked once and then was silent. His restlessness increased and suddenly he was striding across the barnyard and onto the track which led up out of the hollow.

I followed you one day, Anna, he thought. I asked you not to go and you went anyway, and I followed you. He strode on up the hill, his feet making little sound on the beaten track. Much good it did me. You were like an Indian. You turned once and looked behind you. I thought at first that you didn't see me, but you hurried and disappeared over this very hill, and when I got here you were nowhere to be seen.

He surveyed the expanse of red fields linked one to the other by the rail fences and the wild blueberry bushes, remembering that day, and Anna's sturdy figure hurrying away over the crest of the hill, her auburn hair in its neat bun, shining in the sunlight, her back straight in its grey drugget dress.

He strode on. The night air against his skin was as warm as milk. He thought again of the tiny daughter lying beside Anna in the churchyard. We should have had another, and another after that.

He had said as much to her after she had recovered from their daughter's birth, but she had only smiled at him and nodded. She never conceived again, he thought. I had my way with her many times but there was never another one.

He remembered the solid support of her sturdy frame beneath him in their midnight activities. Midnight, because Donald was just a few feet away from them across a thin wall. Belle was always so fragile, he thought, suddenly comparing Anna and his first wife. It's no wonder she couldn't bear children. She was like a sparrow.

Old Annie had attended Belle's delivery, but there was not much she could do except give her wormwood against the pain. The baby was turned, she said. She had tried to turn it but Belle had only screamed in pain and had begged her to stop. Belle had laboured for a day and half and finally died from exhaustion. "The baby was likely dead long before that for the same reason," said Old Annie.

Old Annie knew things. She had the second sight. She also knew about plants and seeds and weeds. She attended Donald's birth too, Ian remembered, and the birth of the nameless little one. Anna seemed to take great comfort in Old Annie's presence after that. She spent many hours visiting her. At least that's where I thought she was, he thought. They say Old Annie knew how to help a woman get with child. I wonder if she knew how to prevent it too? He shivered at the idea. Would Anna have done such a thing? Old Annie's senile now so I guess I'll never know.

His thoughts took him past Murdoch's ruined house, doorless now in the bright moonlight. Old Annie was right about this, too. Murdoch's door was smeared with blood, the blood of the just. My Anna's blood. Though I don't know anymore how just she was. Oh, Anna.

He followed the path that took him across the field to where Anna had lain so few weeks ago. The little pillow of straw, still dark with her blood, lay a few feet into the field, Ian stopped and stared at it. This is all that's left of her, he thought. Rage filled him. Why, Anna? He kicked the straw pillow to bits and began to run, a great lumbering run. It felt good to run again. The soft wind blew past his face and whistled across his ears.

Suddenly he was in James' dooryard. The house was dark and silent now, the windows jagged where Donald had broken them. The rage, which had abated somewhat in his run, returned to a hot boiling fury. "I will burn this house of sin!" he shouted, and ran to the barn to gather some straw. He returned in a few moments with a great armful and stuffed it through the gaping windows, then went back for another. Armload after armload of straw he carried and stuffed through the windows, far more than he needed to start a fire.

"My father helped build this house," he raged, "and I will destroy it!" He stood and surveyed the dark silent house before lighting the match that would burn it to ashes. His father's face seemed to hang in the air before his own, its expression sorrowful. He remembered that expression from his childhood, and hesitated before striking the match. The rage drained away. "Oh, Poppa, what am I to do?" He fell to his knees and wailed like a tiny child, the tears finally coming, awkward, hot and wrenching. He buried his face in his hands and wept, the tears dripping between his work-roughened hands onto his grey homespun shirt. At last, his sorrow and his anger spent, he rose and stumbled away across the moonlit fields to his own place, the match still clutched in his fingers.

"Duncan and Hector found a great deal of straw in James' house yesterday," said Angus. "I saw it myself when I went to see to James' animals. D'you know anything about it, Donald?"

Donald glanced up from the muck he was cleaning out of the gutter and then lowered his eyes again. "No, sir," he replied. He bent busily to his task and seemed to ignore Angus.

"D'you know who would have done it?" Angus looked hard at Donald's face.

Donald looked up and his eyes skewed toward his father then back to his work. "No, sir." He clamped his lips shut and tossed another forkful of manure out the hatch onto the pile.

Angus saw the glance. "It was fresh straw, and would have started a great fire," he observed, "and there was more than enough to do it, too."

"It was me." Ian set the three-legged stool and the bucket beside the cow. "I did it the other night in a fit of rage." He squatted on the stool, clamped the bucket between his knees and began milking. The evening sun shone through the barn door lighting his rugged features.

"I see," said Angus. "That explains it then. What stopped you?"

"I thought of my father and I couldn't do it." He leaned his head into the cow's flank and worked rhythmically at his task. The peace of the task eased some of his tension. He heard the regular working of the cow's jaws as she chewed her cud. Somewhere overhead a mouse rustled in the remains of last year's straw, and the whole was permeated by the sweet smell of warm milk.

Angus pulled up the spare stool and sat down, resting

his back against the door jamb. Presently he said: "Your father built that house."

"Him and a few others."

"You won't be going there again?"

"No. The anger has gone out of me." He sighed. "I only hope that I never see his face again." The anger was back in his voice for a moment. The cow shifted uneasily. "Hold still, bossy."

Angus regarded his friend. "You'll be glad to know, Ian, that it wasn't him that Anna was visiting that night."

Ian looked at him in surprise. "It wasn't? Who was it then?"

"It was Old Annie. Edith MacRae told me this morning. She said Anna was the only one that Old Annie would talk sense to anymore, and that even though Anna may have done all that they said she did, she wasn't doing it that night because she was with Old Annie until late."

"Why didn't she come forward before?"

"She didn't realize the importance of it right away. It was how the ladies were talking about Anna when they were sewing at Mary's the other day that bothered her. No one said a word about how good Anna was to come and keep Old Annie company in the evenings when no one else would. She said that Anna and Old Annie would sit in the parlour and yarn for hours, and when anyone would come in, there wouldn't be a word out of either of them, and pretty soon Anna would say it was time to go and get up and leave without even taking a cup of tea."

"Well, I guess Edith would know since Old Annie lives with her," said Ian. "Annie's her great-aunt on her father's side. She was born on Skye, you know, but she didn't come out with the others."

"I knew they were connected some way, but I didn't think it was that close."

"Anna told me one time."

"It's funny that Anna wouldn't even take a cup of tea with them," said Angus.

"She didn't think that Edith liked her. They had some kind of falling out when they were younger and Anna felt that Edith hadn't forgiven her, so rather than put a strain on Edith to be nice to her, she'd always make some excuse not to stay around her too long."

Angus laughed. "That'd be just like Anna. She never wanted to put anyone out on her own account. Did you hear that Annie walked all the way to my house the other day?"

"No!" Ian looked up at Angus. "I wouldn't think she'd have the strength for that."

"I guess when she has her mind on something she does. Poor little Isabelle was minding her and she couldn't stop her."

"What did Annie have on her mind?"

"Mary said that she wanted awful bad to talk to me. Of course, I was out back and I had enough work there to keep me going until suppertime so I didn't come in until after the ladies had left."

"Did she say what she wanted?"

"Oh, Mary had some tale about Annie knowing who killed Anna, but the rest of it didn't make much sense. She wanders so that it's difficult to know when she is talking sense. She had a little nap on the lounge and when Edith was ready to go home she had to take her home in my wheelbarrow."

Ian laughed. "That wouldn't be much of a ride."

"No, but we put some blankets down and a cushion and she was all right." He rose to leave. "Mary wants you to come to supper some evening soon."

"We will, and thanks," said Ian.

Angus turned and ambled away across the yard.

Ian finished stripping the cow and rose with the bucket of foaming milk in his hand and carried it into the house, where he set it on the shelf in the cool dimness of the porch to allow the cream to rise. He returned to the barn to help Donald finish the chores.

"I'm glad that Angus reminded me of Anna's goodness. It's a strange thing when a man cannot see his own wife as others see her," he said to Donald.

"Nor a son either," said Donald.

Angus walked home that evening through the gathering dusk. The red clay path was dark with dew. Overhead, the first stars shone through the last of the clear sunset, and the moon steadily gained in brightness, already beginning to cast deep shadows all around. In the woods an owl hooted, and then was silent. A dark shadow winged its way overhead, the wind of its passing ruffling Angus' grey hair. It plummeted to earth. A sharp squeak, and the shadow rose again clutching a field mouse in its claws.

It was on a night such as this that Anna was murdered, thought Angus. For all I defended him to Paddy, I hope that Ian had nothing to do with it.

A branch fell in the woods across the brook. Angus started. It was nothing, he reassured himself. He quickened his pace. The noise came again. I still have to go through those woods to get home. I wish I had a stick with me, he thought, trying to calm his heart. He trudged onward. I could go around by Lochie's. It would take me longer, but it would be all open country.

He reached the fork in the track and stopped, still undecided about his route. Mary'll be worried about me if I'm too late. I promised her I'd be back before sunset and it's already past that. I stayed too long at Ian's. He started down the path toward the woods. A creak and another thump, louder than the last, sounded, and Angus retraced his steps and took the path by Lochie's. Mary'll just have to worry.

Murder's a terrible thing, he thought as he swung past Lochie's barnyard. The dog challenged him with bared fangs and a low growl. Angus stopped in his tracks. "Quiet, Buster, it's only me." He held out his hand to the dog. The dog continued to growl.

Lochie came to the door, his bulky figure silhouetted in the door frame by the candle within. "Who's out there?" he shouted over the fierce barking of the dog.

"It's me," replied Angus from the moon shadows by the barn. The dog stopped growling and snuffled around his feet. He pushed it away and trudged across the dooryard.

"Is that you then, Angus?" Lochie peered out into the moon-bright yard. "You're a long way from home."

Angus laughed. "Aye, I was over at Ian's and I stayed too long. I didn't want to walk home through the woods so I came this way."

Lochie sighed. "It's a terrible thing when a man can't even walk out at night without fearing for his life. Will you come in?"

"Not tonight, thanks. I promised Mary I wouldn't be long and I'm already later than I'd planned."

"She'll be worried about you," said Lochie, "and about herself too, no doubt."

"No doubt." Angus turned once again toward home.

I shouldn't be afraid of the likes of James, he scolded himself as he crossed the brook on the stepping stones, his step as agile as it had been when he was thirty. There's hardly any substance to him. And why would he attack me anyway? For that matter, why would he have attacked Anna? He climbed the bank on the other side of the brook, slipping once in the damp clay. Anna was always gentle and kind, a healer, like Old Annie, and even if he had attacked her, she was more than a match for him.

He climbed the little hill on the other side of the brook. In the distance he could see William MacMillan's farmhouse. The candlelight glowed softly from the kitchen window. He'll be reading just now. Angus pictured William poring over the heavy Gaelic Bible, his thick and calloused finger underlining each phrase, his left hand stroking his long brown beard streaked now with grey. Eliza would be sitting in the rocker, rocking gently to and fro, her hands folded in her lap, her thumbs turning one around the other as she stared into the dark shadows in the corners of the kitchen listening to the rise and fall of her husband's voice. It's the only time of the day that she'll be idle, thought Angus.

The light moved, the kitchen darkened, and the light reappeared upstairs. They're off to bed, thought Angus. I wish I was too. He picked up his pace and developed a pain in his shin for his efforts. Drat! He turned around and walked backwards for a short distance. The pain eased. Was that a shadow following him? He stopped. The shadow stopped too. He turned and began to run, his footsteps echoing softly in the night air. The pain in his shin began again and he stopped and turned around. There was no sound and no shadow.

James, James, what have you done to us? I've never been afraid to walk anywhere at night, nor any of my neighbours. Who'd have thought you'd do such a thing?

He turned and trudged on at a slower pace. I remember when you were born, you were tiny even then. Your mother was so sick the whole time she was carrying you that the doctor thought that neither you nor she would live. But you did, and you came to this. And your mother never had another. She'd turn in her grave if she knew what you were up to. It's a good thing she's dead all these years.

He marched onward hardly taking his eyes from the path. I don't want to see shadows in the dark, he thought, and I don't want to run from shadows, either. The path forked and he looked up. The light of home was visible through the trees surrounding his house. The slight sound from his footfalls brought his dog from the barn barking fiercely.

"Be quiet, Dog." The dog's sharp bark of alarm turned to a pleased whining, and he wagged his tail all the way to his ribs in his delight to see his master.

The door opened and Mary stood there, the candle in her hand illuminating the worry lines on her face. "Is it you, Angus?" she asked, peering out into the dooryard.

"It's me." He stepped into the circle of light beside Mary.

"You were a long time coming." She led the way into the kitchen. "I was that worried."

"There were noises in the woods so I came around by Lochie's." He sat down in the rocker and began pulling off his shoes.

"That'd be Rory's cow. I heard Elizabeth say today that she'd escaped and she was that wild they couldn't catch her."

Angus looked up at her and smiled. "And here I thought it was the *bocans*."

"Oh, the *bocans*! The *bocans*! You're as bad as Hector with your talk of spirits." She filled the kettle and set it on the stove with a thump.

"Resist the devil and he shall flee from you."

"Those two have seldom resisted the devil as far as I can see. Maybe it was the two of them that killed poor Anna and made it look like it was James."

"Oh, now Mary, you shouldn't be saying things like that. That's just spreading rumours and gossip. It would be a terrible thing if someone heard you and believed you and charged those two with the deed."

"And who'll hear me in my own kitchen?" She put down the tea to steep and returned the teapot lid with a clang. "Someone's done it, and I don't for a minute believe that it was James, even if he is gone. It could just as well have been those two, or a tramp, or any one of us."

Angus rose and put his arm around her plump shoulders. "Mary, Mary, calm yourself. This'll do you no good." He patted her back.

She flung his arm away, her anger still not spent. "And you! Out walking till all hours of the night! You could have been lying dead and cold just like she was, and I'd not have known till the morning."

"Would that have mattered to you so much?" asked Angus. "I'm an old man now and haven't many more years left. It doesn't really matter how I go, does it?"

Mary stood staring at him. The anger drained from her face leaving only the fear. "Oh, Angus, what would I do without you now?"

"And I without you," said Angus.

"It's the work of the *bocans*," said Hector. He stood staring at the black symbols painted on the walls of James' empty house.

"Or the work of the devil," replied Duncan. "There's evil here. I can feel it."

The two brothers looked at one another, then began to run. Hector looked back once and the early morning sun, just rising over the peak of the roof, seemed to send a bright finger of warning towards him. He turned and began to run even faster.

"Wait for me," Duncan shouted.

"It's the *bocans*, they're after us." Hector tripped over a tree root, regained his balance and hurried on.

"We have to get across water," shouted Duncan as he passed Hector.

"Will a mud puddle do? There's no stream till we get

to William's back field."

"No, it's got to be running water." Duncan cleared James' pasture fence like an experienced hurdler.

"Don't leave me," wailed Hector. He followed Duncan's example at the fence but tripped on the top rail and fell over head first. He lay on the ground gasping and rubbing his right shoulder that had taken the worst of the fall.

"Are you hurt?" Angus' face appeared in silhouette over the top of the fence.

"Don't take me, please don't take me, Mr. *Bocan*. Duncan's much stronger and smarter than I am." Hector's eyes were shut tight and he curled himself into as small a space as he could.

"Och, Hector, what would I want the likes of either of you ?" Angus jumped the fence and reached to help Hector to his feet. Hector wailed and scuttled away from him, covering his head with his arms.

"Hector! Don't be such a *gommach*, it's only me."

Hector opened one eye and peered up at Angus. "Oh, it's you, is it? What're you doing here?"

"I've been coming over to see to James' animals until we could figure out what to do with them." He offered

Hector a hand to help him to his feet. "Where's Duncan?"

"Still running, I expect. He'll probably be across William's creek by now. We thought the *bocans* were after us."

"And you were trying to get across running water. I might have guessed. What were you doing up here anyway?"

Hector rolled his shoulder experimentally and winced at the pain. "The same thing as you were. Tending to James' cows. It's a shame to see good milk go to waste for want of milking. They're almost dry though."

"No, they're not. I just got here before you. You were only getting what was left. I'm late today. What frightened you?"

Hector's face filled with fear. "It was the *bocans*. They've painted evil signs on James' house. It's all written in black. You can go and look but you'll have to go by yourself. I haven't the courage to return." He turned and began a slow progress across the field. "I must go and find Duncan."

Chapter 4

"You will come with me," roared Ian. "You will not insult Mary by refusing her invitation."

"I will not go," shouted Donald. "What do I want to sit around all evening with a bunch of old people for anyway? You'll only talk about my mother."

"And what do you plan to do with your evening?" Ian's voice softened a little.

"Well, someone has to do chores."

"We'll do them before we go," said Ian.

"I'd rather do them myself and not go." Donald recognized his father's softening. "I thought I might chop some wood. It'll soon be getting cold again."

It was now early September, and already the nights weren't as warm as they had been, and the wood did need chopping.

Well, see that you do." Ian turned on his heel and left Donald to his weeding, a job that Anna had always done.

Donald smiled and returned to his task.

"He's that stubborn," lamented Ian to Angus and Mary that evening. "I can't get him to do a thing that he doesn't want to do, and he's too big to punish anymore."

Supper was over and they were sitting around the table enjoying the last of their tea. In the corners of the kitchen the shadows deepened as the setting sun slowly slipped behind the spruces. It was still too early to light the candle. The kettle sang softly to itself on the stove, and the warmth of companionship brought peace to Ian's heart for a little while.

"Well, he is almost a man," agreed Mary.

"He's as big as one anyway," replied Ian. "He's as tall as I am now, and can work just as hard, and him only thirteen."

"You should be proud of him," observed Angus. "He'll be a credit to you yet, and you can't order a man about like you would a child."

"I know, but he's grown up so fast, and now with Anna dying like she did, it's changed him. He's harder somehow, not as biddable."

"Aye, well, a thing like that is bound to change him, he and Anna were so close," said Angus.

"We're all changed by it," said Mary. "I don't think there's one of us in this community that hasn't been touched by it in one way or another, and the fear is the worst of it. Not knowing for sure if it was James that did it, and afraid to walk out alone at night, and wondering if we'll all be killed in our beds."

"I don't think there's any question but that James did it," said Ian. "Why else would he have run, and how would he have known about it?"

"I just don't believe he would do such a thing. They were always so close, even as little children, and he was too much of a dreamer, always quoting poetry and gazing at the stars. It's a wonder he got any work done at all."

"Well, he wasn't much of a farmer," agreed Angus. "He was always the last one to get his crops sown in the spring and the last one to get them harvested in the fall. There was one year there that if we hadn't gone and took it all in hand, he'd have starved and his animals with him."

"He never was much good at reading the weather signs,"

said Ian. "I don't know why he thought he could farm. He'd have made a better clerk, and there was always lots of work in Charlottetown."

"That's what he was doing in Boston, wasn't it?" asked Mary.

"Yes," said Angus, "he had a good job with the bank there, he said."

"It's a pity he had to come home," said Ian.

"Well, he couldn't very well stay away from his own father's funeral," said Angus.

"He should have gone back to Boston, then. I don't know what ever made him think he could be a farmer. His hands were that soft!" said Ian. "And he had no sense for it either. He was a better fiddler than he was a farmer."

"Aye," agreed Mary, "his head was always in the clouds."

"And he still couldn't read the weather," said Angus.

Mary ignored him, her face softening as she remembered James and his adoptive mother, Jean. "He was always such a gentle lad, even when he was little. Jean always said that he had his nose in a book whenever he could get his hands on one. He read all that the schoolmaster would let him borrow, and by the time he was fifteen he was starting in on the minister's library. He could quote poetry by the hour, and the Bible too." She smiled at the memory. "He was very like his father."

Angus looked at her, startled. "His father! Old James couldn't read."

Mary's blush was not discernible in the evening shadows. "I just meant that Poppa James would always be composing poetry, and reciting it any chance he got."

"Humph! Rhymes are more like it, and some of those not too savoury either," said Angus.

"Remember, Ian, the one about Old Annie and the peddler?"

"I do indeed. It wasn't fit for human ears." Ian brightened a little. "He didn't like old Annie, did he?"

"No, he never did, but she attended every one of his wife's birthings, and I think he blamed her for them all being stillborn. James was the only one who lived, and Poppa James never spoke to Old Annie after Jean died with the last one. I don't think he ever forgave her."

"James was such a sweet child. Jean and I were good friends and he always called me Aunt Mary." Mary sighed. "I missed Jean when she went. I miss him too. Every year he brought me the first mayflowers." She sighed again.

"Aye, well, you do bring out the best in others, Mary," said Angus, patting her hand.

It's a Scotch mist that wets an Irishman to the skin, thought Ian as he trudged home that evening. I wonder where Paddy is? He smiled grimly at his own jest, then tripped over a tree root in the dark. "Drat!" he muttered regaining his balance with difficulty in the pitch blackness. "I should have taken Angus' offer of a lantern." He plodded onward. If the murderer is out on a night like this we could pass within two feet of one another and one never see the other, he thought. If he has any sense he'll stay home tonight.

He began to walk down the hill toward home. It's as dark as Egypt out here, I can't even see the lights of home. His feet found the familiar path by feel.

"Donald must have gone to bed. He might have left a light for me," he grumbled under his breath as he felt around on the kitchen table for the candle and fumbled on the mantle shelf for a match. The match flared and the candle brightened the kitchen. Ian climbed the narrow stairs and looked into Donald's room on his way by.

He's not here! Visions of Donald lying dead in the field, felled by a murderer as Anna had been, or lying in a pool of blood in the woodshed, a victim of the axe he was using to chop wood, flashed through his mind. He hastened downstairs and lighted a lantern. The mist had turned to rain, and the raindrops hissed against the hot lantern sides. He hurried to the wood house as fast as the darkness would let him and lifting the light high, he peered into the gloom. The wood was neatly stacked along the wall, the floor, spongy with years of wood chips, was covered with the fresh chips from Donald's axe. Donald wasn't there.

Ian hurried to the barn. "Donald! Donald! Are you there?" He flung open the door. The barn, too, was empty, except for the cow, which turned an enquiring soft brown eye toward Ian and belched another cud. Somewhere in the darkness overhead a small night creature rustled in the hay. The warm dustiness of the barn surrounded the peace within its walls. Raindrops pattered on the roof. Ian shivered.

"Donald! Donald! Are you there, Donald?" He climbed the ladder into the loft, the glow from his lantern illuminating the cobwebs and hay. A scurry of tiny feet was his only answer.

"Drat that boy," he grunted as he climbed down from the loft. "Where could he have gotten to?" He stood for a moment thinking. The yellow barn cat wound around his legs and mewed hopefully for a sip of milk. Ian pushed her away. Outside the rain came down even harder. "I hope he has sense enough to get in out of this deluge." He stood staring out into the drowned blackness of the yard. Presently the downpour lessened and he made his way back across the yard, now slimy with mud.

I'd better light the fire. Donald'll be soaked when he gets home, and likely cold too. He stirred up the ashes with the poker. There was not even a spark. He rummaged in the wood box and found some chips and kindling and stacked them in the firebox. The match flared and the kindling caught. He added a couple of sticks, and the fire began to warm the room. He flung himself into the rocker and closed his eyes.

I never knew grief was such a heavy thing, he thought. It's like a ton weight on my shoulders, a greyness in my mind, and it won't move. I loved her even more than I loved Belle, he thought in surprise. I don't deserve this. And now

Donald's gone, and I don't know where he is. Ian stared through the spaces in the stove draft and watched the flicker of the fire on the ashes as it grew and consumed the wood in the firebox above. *At least wherever he is, he can't have been gone long. There's enough wood there to last a week.* He leaned his head back and his breathing deepened and presently he slept. Outside, the rain poured down again.

He was awakened at midnight by a slight noise, more an awareness of movement than real sound. He stirred and opened his eyes. Donald was on his way up to bed.

Ian blinked and raised his head, wincing at the crick in his neck. The fire had almost burnt itself out and the dampness in the seams of his shirt was uncomfortable.

"And where were you?" he asked out of the shadows of the kitchen.

Donald jumped and stopped his stealthy climb up the narrow stairs. "Out." He did not turn to face his father.

"Come down here and look at me when you speak!"

Donald climbed down to the kitchen again. He stood in front of Ian but did not look at him. He was soaked to the skin, his dark hair, made even darker by the rain, stuck in loose ringlets to his skull. He shivered.

"Where have you been in this weather?" Ian rose and stoked up the fire again.

"I told you, out."

"Out is not a sufficient answer." Ian ignored Donald's tone. "Where out?"

Donald shrugged one shoulder. "Out walking."

Ian handed him a towel. "You're soaked. You'll catch your death of pneumonia. This is not fit weather to be walking in."

"It wasn't raining when I left." Donald rubbed at his dripping hair.

"And where did you go?" Ian stared hard at his son.

"Just walking." He mopped his face and sniffed.

"I don't suppose you walked past James', did you?"

"I might have, I don't remember."

"You must remember where you walked," said Ian. "You're too young to be that forgetful."

"All right, I went past there, but I didn't go in." Donald gave Ian a dirty look. "When it started to rain I holed up in Murdoch's old place hoping it would pass, but it didn't."

"I can't imagine that Murdoch's place would afford much protection from the storm."

"It leaks, but it's better than nothing. I tried for home between downpours, but I didn't make it." He sneezed. "Can I go to bed now?"

It stopped raining in the night and the next morning dawned bright with the ecstatic bubbling song of the bobolink and the rapid cu-cu-cu of the cuckoo bird. Somewhere in the woods a woodpecker tapped out his breakfast from a birch tree. A fresh salt breeze blew in from the Northumberland Strait. White powder puff clouds floated in the blue immensity of the sky and the world seemed freshly painted in bright colours.

A lovely September day, thought Ian as he and Donald walked to church. School will be starting again tomorrow, it will be good for Donald to be among the young again. Perhaps he'll be less sullen.

Donald sneezed.

"So you've caught cold from last night's escapade," said Ian.

Donald sniffed hugely and didn't reply.

Ian handed him a clean handkerchief. "You know, Donald, our life together will be much pleasanter if you would show a little courtesy."

"Yes, sir," sniffed Donald and blew his nose. He handed the handkerchief back to his father.

"Keep it," said Ian, "you need it worse than I do."

"Thanks." He sniffed again.

They removed their hats as they entered the church. It's hard to believe that she's been gone more than a month already, thought Ian, the lightening of his spirits of a moment before sliding away from him at the remembrance. He bowed his head, the crick in his neck from the night before not quite gone. Presently the precentor announced the first hymn and everyone rose.

The precentor chose a pitch. "Unto the hills, around do I lift up my longing eyes." The congregation straggled into the tune, the melody rose and fell, all voices great and small interweaving and creating a cloth more beautiful than its individual strands. The Psalm meandered to a close and they all remained standing for the prayer.

The next hymn, the scripture reading, and the offering passed and Ian hardly noticed them, rising when the others did and sitting when they sat. Donald sneezed occasionally and sniffed frequently, even with vigorous applications of his father's handkerchief to his streaming nose. Sunlight glancing off Mr. MacDonald's watch as he checked the time before beginning the sermon roused Ian from his reverie and the pew creaked as he cautiously changed his position.

"The text today is from Matthew 10, verses 26 and 29 to 31."

> Fear them not therefore: for there is nothing covered, that shall not be revealed; and hid, that shall not be known.... And are not two sparrows sold for a farthing? and one of them shall not fall on the ground without your Father. But the very hairs of your head are all numbered. Fear ye not therefore, ye are of more value than many sparrows.

He paused and drew breath, looking calmly out over the congregation. "There is a terrible fear abroad these days," he began. "A terrible thing has been done in our midst and we are all afraid to walk out alone. But we are not alone. We are never alone, for the Lord walks with us every step of the way."

"I wonder where He was when Anna was on her way home," whispered Duncan.

"Maybe she was moving too fast and he couldn't keep up," suggested Hector under his breath.

Angus stared them both into silence, then turned his attention back to the sermon.

The congregation became increasingly restive toward the end of the hour. From the women's side of the church the children whined and mothers quieted them as unobtrusively as they could. Donald sneezed and swabbed at his nose with the now sodden handkerchief. Duncan commented to Hector more than once despite Angus' attempts to maintain order by eye contact alone. The soft rustle of a paper bag sounded throughout the sanctuary as a woman passed her peppermints to her neighbours. From his seat with the elders William glared down at her, but she didn't see. The September sun warmed the room and presently Alexander's soft snores rose and fell until his head dropped onto his chest and he awoke with a start.

"And so you see," said Mr. MacDonald, "that since we are more important than the sparrows, and He cares a great deal for the sparrows, we need never fear. Let us pray."

"A fine sermon, Mr. MacDonald," said Alexander shaking the minister's hand and stifling a yawn.

"A very timely sermon," said William. "We've taken to locking our doors at night."

"And in the daytime too," chirped Eliza, sticking out

a bird-like hand to the minister. "It was, indeed, a timely sermon, but I think, until the culprit is caught, I'll continue to lock my door." She turned away down the steps.

"I didn't know you locked the door in the daytime too," said William following after her. "There's no need of that. How will I get in?"

"Good morning, Mr. MacDonald," said Ian, as usual the last to leave the church. Donald slipped past him with a very brief good morning to the minister, and hurried to join the other boys. Ian held out his hand to shake hands with the minister. "It was a fine sermon, and one we needed to hear."

"Good morning, Mr. Gillis. Kind words, I'm sure. It's hard to know what to say in times like these. Everyone's so ill at ease, even with his own neighbours, and while the greatest loss was yours, we've lost something very precious in the community as well. I don't know if we'll ever get it back."

"Aye, well, we've certainly lost the trust of each other," replied Ian, "and that will be a hard thing to regain."

"We've lost our innocence too, and I don't think we'll ever get that back even if they catch the devil who did this a dozen times over. The trust will come back eventually, for we're all family and neighbours. By the way, I see young Donald has acquired quite a cold from sitting out in the rain last night."

Ian's eyes narrowed. "Sitting out in the rain? When was this?"

"I was called out to Old Annie last night and I saw him in the graveyard over by Anna's grave. Old Annie is trying to die for the third time. Edith says she has something on her mind but she won't or can't tell her what."

"Won't is probably more like. Old Annie has secrets on everyone here. She's been around almost since the start."

"I wasn't very long at Edith's because by the time I got there, Old Annie was rambling again. On my way over I'd thought of another point that I wanted to make in my sermon today, so I just came right back. I was only gone about an hour or so. By the time I was coming back it was pouring rain and had been for some time, but there was Donald still sitting by Anna's grave soaked to the skin."

"Are you sure it was him? It was an awful dark night."

"It was him. I walked over to him and tried to get him to come in with me or go home, not to be sitting out like that getting cold and wet, but he just shook me away and wouldn't move. I tried again to persuade him, but he got angry and called me a foul name."

"That's very unlike him. I've never known him to use bad language. He was taught better than that. I'll speak to him." Ian stared across the yard to where Donald was standing on the periphery of a group of boys looking very morose. "If that's what he's been up to, it's no wonder he's sick."

"I fear he's taking Anna's death much harder than we realize. It's almost time for him to stop grieving so deeply and take up life again."

"Och, he's at that difficult age. He's not a child anymore, but he's not quite a man either, and hasn't had much practice at being a man. School's starting again tomorrow, maybe that'll help him settle down. Good day, Mr. MacDonald."

Ian turned toward the boys and started across the churchyard. Donald saw him coming and an expression of fear crossed his face as he tried to hide himself among the others.

"Donald. It's time we were going. Say good-bye to your friends now, and come home with me."

Donald eased his way out from behind Rory and went to his father and together they turned toward home.

The clear brightness of the morning sun was mellowing into the golden light of an early autumn noon as they made their way down the track. Ian hummed the closing hymn under his breath. He was slightly off pitch. Presently he said, "So you weren't just out last night I hear."

Donald didn't reply.

"I am speaking to you," roared Ian. "And I will have an answer."

"Yes, sir," muttered Donald between set teeth, then sneezed.

"Well, I'm waiting!"

"I went to visit Momma's grave." Donald sniffed a long sniff. "What's wrong with that?"

"Why couldn't you have told me that last night?"

"Don't I have a right to some privacy?"

"Privacy? Privacy!" Ian almost shouted. "You're only a child yet. What do you want with privacy?"

"No, Poppa. I'm thirteen, nearly fourteen. I do a man's work. I am almost a man." He sniffed hugely and sneezed again.

"You're a child," bellowed Ian. "Only children sit out in the rain catching their death of cold, and until you can behave responsibly, I shall consider you a child. Good heavens, you don't even shave yet."

"Oh, but I do, and I have done for the past eight months. Momma bought me a razor that day she went to the store during the January thaw last winter, and I've been using it ever since." He scrubbed at his nose with the soggy handkerchief.

Ian looked more closely at his son. There was a faint shadowing on his jaw and across his upper lip that he had never noticed before. "Well! Well, shaving doesn't make you a man, behaviour does, and until you behave like one you're still a child. By the way, I don't ever want to hear of you using foul language again either. Especially not to the minister. He's a good man and deserves better than that. You'll go over this afternoon and apologize to him." He strode away down the path.

It's one more thing I didn't know about Anna, he thought, and now I'm fighting with our son about it. He thought back to the day last January when winter had released its cold grip on the Island for a brief few days before covering it with another thick blanket of snow. She was that bright and cheery that day, he remembered. She was right eager to get to the store, before the weather closed in again, she said. I thought she had a secret then, but she never told me about it and I forgot to ask her, and when she came home, the secret seemed even bigger between her and Donald. I asked her then, what was going on, but she was full of gossip from Mrs. John, as if that was all it was. His angry pace brought him home in no time. It's not that I mind that she did that for him, he thought, but she might have told me about my own son.

Chapter 5

Sunday afternoon crept onward, its oppressive silence barely alleviated by the bright sunshine outdoors. Donald had been sent to make his apologies to Mr. MacDonald, and Ian sat in the rocker by the cold stove and tried to read, his big calloused finger passing slowly beneath the words as he grappled with each syllable.

> Oh that my grief were thoroughly weighed, and my calamity laid in the balances together! For now it would be heavier than the sand of the sea: therefore my words are swallowed up. For the arrows of the Almighty are within me, the poison whereof drinketh up my spirit: the terrors of God do set themselves in array against me.

"Indeed, I am like Job," he mourned. "My wife is dead by another's hand, the murderer is still undiscovered, and my son defies me daily." He leafed the thin pages. His finger stopped, still in Job. Anna was so much better at this than I am. She had such a lovely flow to her voice when she read the Bible to us. She made the stories come alive somehow, and I can't even get the sense of the words very well. He tried again.

> Men groan from out of the city, and the soul of the wounded crieth out: yet God layeth not the folly to them. They are of those that rebel against the light; they know not the ways thereof, nor abide in the paths thereof. The murderer rising with the light killeth the poor and needy, and in the night as a thief. The eye of the adulterer waiteth for the twilight, saying, No eye shall see me: and disguiseth his face.

"Are you home, Ian?" called Angus from the doorway.

Ian set down his Bible, and went to the door. "Aye, come in, Angus. I was just trying to read a bit, but it's no use. I'm not good at it. I'm much better at reciting the verses from memory, but I don't have any from heart for these sad times, and with Anna gone it may be too late to learn any more." He ushered Angus into the kitchen. "Pull up a chair."

"You look very downcast. What were you reading?"

"I opened to Job. Anna always did that if she was troubled. She said that the Lord would lead her to the right verse."

"Well, Job's enough to make anyone downcast, why didn't you try to open to Psalms? There's more encouragement there." Angus cleared his throat and began to recite, "God is our refuge and strength, a very present help in trouble."

Ian sighed. "I do need help, for I don't understand. Anna was the centre of this household, and now she's gone, and I don't know why, and my son is defying me at every turn, and anyone else who has anything to say to him." He buried his head in his hands and moaned aloud. "Who has done this terrible thing to us, for I cannot believe that it was James."

Angus cleared his throat. "If it's any comfort to you, Ian, I don't think it was James either, for he loved Anna as much as you did, and I don't think he had it in him to do it."

Ian mopped his face with his handkerchief. "It must have been a stranger then, for none of our neighbours would do such a thing either."

The two men rocked in silence for a few minutes, each lost in his own thoughts about Anna. Presently Angus said: "There's been mischief done up at James' house."

"What kind of mischief?" Ian closed the Bible and set it on the table.

"Someone painted signs on it."

"Well, it wasn't me. What kind of signs?"

"I didn't think it was you." Angus looked at Ian squarely. "They were just symbols, nothing I could identify. It was Hector and Duncan who found them."

"I suppose they thought it was the *bocans* who did it."

"They did. They were running for their lives across James' cow pasture looking for some running water. Hector tripped on the top rail of the fence and fell over. It's a wonder he didn't kill himself." Ian chuckled. "Those two are enough to make the crows laugh." He shook his head. "They'll be the death of one another yet." His smile faded. "Who d'you suppose did the painting?"

Angus shrugged. "Who knows. It might have been some prank or other that the children were up to. It could have been tramps."

"The peddler was around the other day. He took a fancy to Anna the first time he came here and he always brought her a little trinket, but I doubt he'd have the sense to do something like that."

"Probably not, but he did like Anna awfully well."

Angus tugged at his lower lip. "Mm, perhaps." The two men were silent for a few minutes. Presently Angus asked: "What's Donald up to today?"

Ian frowned. "He's gone off to Mr. MacDonald's to apologize for a rudeness to him from last night."

"He has a terrible cold. I felt sorry for him in church today, sniffing and sneezing."

"It serves him right. That young imp sat out in the rainstorm at his mother's grave last night. He came home at midnight soaked to the skin and shivering."

"That was a daft thing to do. You'd think he'd have sense enough to come home when it started to rain."

"And him supposed to be so grown up according to him. Mr. MacDonald said he was there when he went to visit Old Annie last night, and he was still there when he came back, and it was pouring rain all that time."

"Tch, tch," clucked Angus. "He'll be coming down with pneumonia if he's not careful."

"Yes, and only me to nurse him," grumbled Ian. "And he's getting that saucy. Mr. MacDonald said that he called him a bad name last night. I could hardly believe it. He was brought up better than that. His mother would turn over in her grave if she knew. I sent him over to beg his pardon right after we had dinner. I told him not to come back until he'd done so."

"Well, in that case, he may not be back, for I just saw him over with Lochie's Neil by his barn. I don't think he was anywhere near the manse this afternoon, though he may go yet."

"Drat that boy! Why won't he do what he's told? What am I going to do with him?"

"I'm not a good one to say, not having any of my own. I suspect he's just still grieving and it will pass soon."

"The sooner, the better, then."

The two men were silent for a long moment.

"Have you heard?" asked Angus presently. "Lochie's clearing another field. Him and Neil cut the trees last month while Neil was off school, and they're having a stumping next Saturday."

"Well, now, I remember him saying he was going to. I didn't realize that he'd already done it. He'll be a rich man before he dies, with all that land."

"As long as he's able to work it. It takes a long time and

a great effort to clear a piece of land fit for ploughing, and there were a lot of trees on it. He got enough wood off it to do him for the next five years."

"He could build a barn with that much wood," said Ian.

"He'll need to if the farm gets much bigger."

"Well, he has Neil to help him. He's almost as big as his father these days."

"Yes, he's almost a man. He'll be a good farmer like his father and his grandfather before that. They could grow anything."

"They grow up so fast," agreed Ian. "Donald informed me today that he's been shaving these last eight months."

"No! And he didn't tell you before this?"

Ian shook his head. "It was Anna that got him the razor last spring and never said a word about it."

"And you never noticed?"

"No, and I'm beginning to think there was a lot I didn't notice. I was happy and going about my business, and I never thought to observe either of them too closely. They both seemed contented enough."

"Aye, well, who can fathom the ways of women? Even my Mary has her little secrets, things that she doesn't tell me, you know. I always figured they were harmless enough, but maybe I should question her a little more closely. Although that would seem like prying, and might not be respectful. Mary's a good sensible woman."

Ian sighed. "It's so hard to know what's right. I gave Anna all the freedom she seemed to want, and look what it did for her. Maybe I should have been stricter with her."

"Well, you know what they say about hindsight and foresight."

"G'day Lochie. Alexander. It's a fine day. Where's Neil this morning?" Ian leaned on his stumping hoe as the other two were doing and looked around. "It's a big field you're planning, Lochie."

"That was Neil's doing," said Lochie. "Two thirds this size would have done, but he insisted that he wanted a field bigger than the brook pasture. He's just finishing chores now."

"We'll let him clear a few stumps, and he may be willing to let the rest grow up to woods again," said Alexander.

The others laughed.

"Where's Donald? I thought he'd be with you,"

asked Lochie.

"He'll be along. He's still suffering with that cold he caught last week. He's been that cross and hard to get along with, I left him to finish the milking by himself."

"Well, here's Angus with Duncan and Hector. G'day, g'day!" Alexander greeted them. "We can get started now." He picked up his hoe. "Which one'll we tackle first?"

"We'll start with these four here, I guess," said Lochie. "That'll give us a sense of accomplishment before we get to those three big ones over there."

"We'll need that," said Angus. "Those are the biggest stumps I've ever seen. They must be six feet across."

"They've been there for a long time," said Lochie. "I remember them from when I was a lad. I hated to cut them down." He swung at a root with his hoe, and grunted as the hoe made contact.

"You could have left them." Angus raised his hoe to follow Lochie.

"They were old and ready to fall. Besides, they were in a bad place."

"Did you get much lumber out of them?" asked Alexander tackling the roots on the other side of the tree stump. He pried at the root where it narrowed into smaller branches and disappeared underground.

"Not much," grunted Lochie. "The small stuff was only fit for firewood. Those three big ones were the only ones that were straight enough to be of any use. I thought I might keep them and build an addition to the square barn." He swung again. "Drat! I missed that pesky thing." He swung again and the red dirt flew.

"You'll need it." Angus struggled with a stubborn root. "I suppose you plan to plant this in grain?"

"No, potatoes." Lochie wiped his streaming face. "They're fetching a good price just now and if we don't get this field all cleared this fall, I can still plant around the stumps."

"It's a shame about the lumber." Alexander's breath came in gasps. "I heard they were laying the keel for a fancy boat for a rich American next week and they were calling for good lumber." He stopped to catch his breath. "Here Duncan, you and Hector dig for awhile."

"We're working on this one," said Duncan. "We've got it almost cleared." A stream of tobacco juice emphasized his words, narrowly missing Hector's shoes.

"Watch where you're spittin', you great *groik*!" Hector polished the toe of his shoe against the back of his trouser leg.

"Well, get out of the way of where I'm spittin'." Duncan worked vigorously on his chew. He ambled over to where Angus had been working. "You fellows are doing a fine job. I couldn't do any better myself."

"Try." Angus sat down on a nearby stump. "I'll go and get the horse from William and see if he's coming over, as soon as I've caught my breath."

"Never mind," said Lochie, "here's William and Eliza now. " He leaned on his hoe, his face red from his exertions. "G'day William. Eliza. Whatever you've got in your basket smells some good. The ladies are all at the house."

Eliza greeted the men, then continued on toward the house, the fragrance of her basket lingering on the air after her passing. She hurried down the path, oblivious to the beauty of the fall day. A light frost in the hollows the night before had encouraged the leaves into their autumn colours, and most of them now were bright shades of yellow and red. It was still too early for many to have fallen, so the little hollow where Lochie's house stood looked as if it were surrounded by bright pillows, the harvested fields beyond were blankets of red. The air was fresh and a little cold. The smell of wood smoke from Lochie's fireplace was a reminder of the approach of winter. In the distance, through a gap in the trees, the bright blue waters of the Northumberland Strait sparkled in the sunlight. Lochie's dog bounded up to Eliza, his tail rotating like a windmill, his mouth gaping into a silly grin.

"You're not much of a watchdog." She rapped on the door.

The dog whined and licked her hand.

"Get away, dog!" She stamped her foot, and the dog sat down on the edge of the sandstone step to watch her. "Are you home, Mary?" she called through the open door.

"Here's Eliza now," said Mary. "C'mon in Eliza, we're all here." She held the door for her. "My, something smells good. How were the men getting along when you went by?"

"Duncan and Hector were the only two who seemed to be working."

"For a change." Edith laughed. "Those two would do anything to get out of a little work. I'm surprised they even got them to pick up a shovel."

"Well, I think the others had already done their own share and were taking a break. Angus looked kind of wilted just then." She set her basket on the table. "Everything went wrong this morning. I slept later than usual and I wanted to set bread this morning before we came over, and I didn't get that done, so I made a couple of bonnicks. They'll have to do. I'll make another tonight for the Sabbath. It won't hurt William to do without bread for one day. He's always so fussy."

She began unpacking her basket. "I made an apple pie yesterday. I thought it might be good to have, and we have a ton of those nice red apples all just ready to fall off the trees. You'd all better come and help yourselves to them before the frost gets them. I've already picked all that we can use." She lifted a jar of green tomato chow out of the basket. "I did up these last month. They're awful good, if I do say so myself." She pulled a clean apron from the bottom of the basket and set the empty basket on the floor. "There now, what can I do to help?"

"Nothing for now," said Rachael Cameron. "I peeled the potatoes and left them in water last night, and I just finished the carrots and turnips. The roast is in the oven since six o'clock this morning so everything should be ready on time. We were just having a gossip and a cup of tea." A squawk from the corner interrupted her words.

"I see you brought Old Annie, Edith," said Eliza.

"Well, I wanted to come, and she can't be left by herself any more. A few minutes is all she's safe for, so Allan put her in the hand cart and we pulled her over on that. She weighs next to nothing now. He could just about have carried her."

"It'd be a long walk if he was carrying her, even so."

"How old is she now?" asked Flora.

"We don't really know," replied Edith, "she came over just after the first group of settlers, and she was a young woman then, and that's over forty years ago. She used to tell us about the old country and the trip over when she still had her mind."

"I heard she was married at one time." Catherine knitted vigorously on a sock.

"I think she was. She said once that he died on the way over and was buried at sea. At least I think that's who she meant, though it could have been a brother. I was never too clear on that. At any rate, she never had any children, and no way of getting back to Scotland even if she had wanted to go."

"She didn't want to?" asked Catherine. "Why would she want to stay here with no close family around?"

"She was a midwife and knew the value of herbs and roots, and they needed her here. Besides, there was nothing to go back to except poverty and persecution, and she was a woman alone," said Edith. "You never wanted to go back to Scotland, did you Annie?" She reached over and brushed a few wisps of white hair out of Annie's faded blue eyes.

Annie looked at her blankly for a moment. "Scotland?" she asked.

"Yes, to Kilmaluagh."

"Oh, Kilmaluagh." Her forehead wrinkled into an unhappy frown. "Alistair." A tear formed and slipped over her short grey lashes. "Alistair."

"Who's Alistair, Annie?" asked Edith.

Annie didn't reply. "Alistair," she whispered.

Edith tried to call her back. "Annie, who's Alistair?"

"Bonny man," said Annie. "Alistair," she mourned.

"Was Alistair your husband?" Edith stroked Annie's wrinkled hand.

"He should have been." Annie lapsed into silent weeping. Tears dripped off her withered chin.

"What happened to him?"

Annie rocked back and forth in her chair. "Died and then they drowned him. So much death then, so much death now, and my own is coming, I can see it coming. It gets closer every day." She clamped her lips shut, and drifted back into her wandering mind, still rocking.

The kitchen was in silence. Flora cleared her throat. "Well, that's some story. I wonder if it's true?"

"It's close enough," said Mary. " She told me a little of it years ago, and it was similar to that, although she never did tell me much about Alistair, not even his name. I gathered then that there was some secret about their relationship, and Annie was always very good at keeping secrets. I was surprised she even told me that."

Catherine's knitting needles clicked. "It's a funny thing that no one else ever spoke of it. You'd think that someone would have said something over the years."

"Perhaps they didn't know," said Flora. "If she was that good at keeping secrets …" Her voice trailed away.

"Well, whatever the story was, she didn't want anyone

to know about it, and probably still doesn't," said Mary, "and I don't think it's up to us to pry into her affairs."

"I agree," said Rachael. "Anyway, it's time we were getting dinner on, the men'll be in in about an hour, and likely starving hungry." She got to her feet. "I'll just start the potatoes and the vegetables. Flora, you and Mary can start setting the table. " She bustled off into the pantry.

Thumps and laughter heralded the men's arrival in the porch an hour or so later, and presently they all trooped into the kitchen.

"It smells good in here, Rachael," said Alexander.

"It'll be good to have a woman's cooking again for a change," said Ian. "I'm fair sick of my own these days."

"Sit in then, and have your dinner," said Rachael, "we'll eat when you've all finished." She set a plate of Eliza's *bannoch* on the table. "How much did you get done this morning?"

"Five small ones and one of the big ones. We've already started on the second big one. I think the roots must go all the way to China." He pulled up a chair to the head of the table. "Sit in, everyone. William, will you return thanks?"

Heads bent as William asked the blessing. "For what we are about to receive may we be truly grateful, and pardon our sins, in Jesus' name, Amen."

"Help yourselves, then," said Rachael, "and don't be shy, there's plenty for all of us. Alexander, you can start the potatoes, and Lochie, you start the meat."

The kitchen was silent except for the scrape of knives and forks against plates, noisy blowing to cool hot tea, and noisier sipping to get it past tender tongues without scorching.

Presently Ian said: "This is wonderful, Rachael. The best meal I've had since I was at Angus' the other week."

"I had plenty of help today," said Rachael. "Any one for a little pie?"

"I see you brought Annie with you, Edith," said Alexander, swallowing his last bite.

"Yes, she's too forgetful to leave by herself anymore, and she's not really any trouble to take with us if we're not going too far."

He pulled his rumpled handkerchief out of his hip pocket and blew his nose, then mopped at his moustache, yellowed by years of tea and tobacco. "She must be about ninety by now, isn't she?"

"We were thinking this morning that she was closer to seventy. She wasn't a young woman when she came here."

"My own father said one time that she was over thirty when she immigrated," said Alexander. "He didn't know by how much. Of course, he could have been mistaken, he was just a young fellow himself. He said that all the children were afraid of her because she had the second sight, and that she could foresee death. They used to say that you didn't want to look her in the eye for too long." He filled his pipe and struck a match. Clouds of smoke issued forth as he puffed to get the pipe going to his satisfaction.

"Why not?" asked Flora.

"Because she'd be apt to tell you something you didn't want to hear," said Alexander through the fog from his pipe. "I remember old Angus Shaw. He met her on the way to church one morning and she told him that in the time of the blue moon he'd be sorrowing, and that month there was another full moon and his wife gave birth to a baby that was deformed. It was a boy and the only one they ever had, and he couldn't live. It broke both of their hearts. He was so set on having a son after having five daughters. It aged Isabelle before her time and she never had another. They're both dead now, these thirty years." He puffed in silence for awhile looking over at Annie who seemed to be asleep in her chair by the stove.

Presently she sighed and opened her eyes looking directly at Ian. "Ian Gillis, is that you?" she quavered. "Come here, I want you."

Ian's face paled and he rose from his seat and went to stand in front of Annie. "What is it you want, Annie?"

"Come here," she whispered, crooking a withered finger at him.

Ian bent his head close to Old Annie, and she whispered softly into his ear. The kitchen was as still as an empty church, as the others strained to hear and failed. Ian's face went paler yet, and he backed away from Annie, then turned and hurried back to his seat.

"What did she say to you, man? You're as white as a sheet!" said William.

"Nothing, nothing," mumbled Ian. "She's just a crazy old woman."

❖

Eliza was the first to break the silence after the men left. "I wonder what in the world Annie said to Ian?" She picked up the last stack of dirty dishes to carry them to the pantry.

"It must have been something dreadful, for I've never seen a man go as white in the face as he did just then," said Rachael.

"Well, there've certainly been strange goings on at his house these past few months," replied Catherine. "I wouldn't be surprised at all, at all, if she told him something about who murdered Anna."

"But Old Annie doesn't have any idea what's going on any more," protested Edith," and I should know, it's me that looks after her."

"Well, you never know," replied Catherine, "my Aunt Mary didn't know a thing for years before she died if you asked her, but she could tell the whole world your business if she had a mind to."

"So the story she told about you and John MacKenzie was true then, was it?" Rachael's eyes twinkled merrily.

"It certainly was not!" Catherine's knitting needles clicked faster than ever. "He came that day to see Poppa about helping him with the threshing. He hardly ever said a word to me."

"He must have done something." Rachael enjoyed Catherine's discomfort. "Otherwise your Aunt Mary wouldn't have had anything to say."

"Well, he didn't" snapped Catherine, "and Aunt Mary wasn't Old Annie either."

"I wonder what Annie did say to Ian?" said Mary.

"She probably told him the plain truth about Anna," retorted Catherine. "Maybe she even told him who did it."

"Now Catherine," said Mary, "that's no way talk about Anna. She was our neighbour, and a good one she was too. She'd be the first one there if there was any trouble."

"She was probably feeling guilty for all her sinning when she wasn't there," sniffed Catherine. "If all the stories about her are true, she got what was coming to her."

"Catherine! No one deserves to be murdered," chorused the others.

"Especially not my mother," said Donald from the doorway. "May I have a clean bucket for water, please, Mrs. Cameron. Duncan set the bucket down too near the horse and Hector backed the horse up and he stepped on it."

"Trust Duncan and Hector to get into something."

Rachael shook her head. "Those two never get anything right." She took the remains of the water bucket from Donald. "There's another one hanging by the well. Take it."

"Thank you." Donald disappeared out the door.

"I guess I'd better save these pieces, Lochie may be able to mend them," she said.

"I wonder how long he was standing there?" said Mary.

"I didn't see him come in."

"That child gets around like a cat." Catherine exploded. "He's as sly as his mother ever thought of being."

"Now Catherine," said Eliza, "it may be true that his mother was sly, but he's only a child yet, he has nothing to be sly about."

Catherine sniffed. "You mark my words, he'll be in trouble yet."

"Oh, Catherine," teased Rachael, "now you're sounding like Annie. Didn't I hear you were related to her a few generations back?"

"Indeed not," replied Catherine, "there's never been any witches in the Finlayson clan, nor the second sight either."

❖

Angus paused in his steady stride to take in the view from the top of the rise. The sun had just set, leaving the horizon a clear golden green. Overhead the first stars of the evening were becoming visible. The moon had not yet risen. The smell of frost was in the air.

It'll be a cold one tonight, thought Angus. I'm glad I kept the calf in. The banking's done, so it won't be so cold on the feet in the morning. He tucked his scarf closer to his throat. It won't do to get a cold now, it'll last all winter.

To the left lay Catherine Finlayson's house, hidden in its grove of trees. Only the barns and the hay barracks were visible from where he stood. Behind them was a small apple orchard gone wild from lack of care.

It's too bad Catherine couldn't keep the orchard. Her father had lovely apples from it. They made the best cider. Her mother made grand pies too.

Farther on and to the right lay the end of Ian's lane. A movement caught Angus' attention. I wonder if that was Ian or Donald? They'd hardly be finished chores yet. The shadow moved and changed shape. It's too small for either of them, thought Angus. I wonder what it is? The shadow dissolved into the encroaching darkness. The night was as silent as it had ever been. The sound of cats crying came from the direction of Catherine's barnyard, carried clearly on the frosty air.

Those cats sound in distress, thought Angus, as the cries became more urgent and sorrowful. He stepped off the track into Catherine's lane and hurried toward her barnyard.

Two small figures were busy with a cord and two half-grown cats.

"Hurry, Rory, she'll hear us."

"I can't go any faster, my fingers are cold."

"Here, let me do it. You hold them. Be careful though, that big one scratches awful."

"Well, the little one bites. Are you soon done?"

"I'm done. Put them over the clothesline and be quick about it."

The squalling of the tied cats increased as they fought one another to get free. Little Rory and James stood back to observe their handiwork. "I guess that's worth tuppence," said James.

Angus' large hands descended one on each of the boys' shoulders. He turned the boys around to face him. "Who put you boys up to this?" The shrieking of the cats got louder and more frantic. Angus let go of the children and began to untangle the knot in the cord that held the two cats by their tails face to face across the clothes line.

"Run!" shouted James.

"You will not run." Angus' voice stopped them both in their tracks. "I asked you, who put you up to this evil thing?"

"No one, sir. We just did it ourselves." Little Rory's pale blue gaze did not quite meet the directness of Angus' own dark blue eyes.

"James? Is that true?" The knots gave way and the two cats leaped to the ground and disappeared into the darkness, snarling and spitting. Angus turned to face the two culprits.

"Y-yes," stammered James in response to a poke in the ribs from Little Rory.

"You know that it's sinning if you tell a lie," said Angus, "and you know what happens to sinners."

"T-they go to hell?" said James.

"So Reverend MacDonald tells me. And you know what they say." Angus turned his fierce dark gaze on Rory.

"No, sir." Little Rory's bravado was failing him.

"They say, 'be sure your sins will find you out.' D'you understand what that means?"

"N-no, sir." There was a quaver in Rory's voice now.

"It means, Little Rory, that when you do something sinful, that sooner or later someone discovers it, never mind that God always knows what you're up to. Now I'm going to ask you again, who put you up to this?"

"Donald did." James' voice was on the edge of tears. "He said we wouldn't get caught, and that it would be ever so much fun to see those two cats fighting across the clothes line."

"He even paid us tuppence each to do it," offered Rory.

"And did you think it was a right thing to do?"

Both Rory and James shrugged. "It seemed like fun at the time." James scuffed his bare foot in the grass.

"Well, it was cruel. You don't ever treat an animal like that. Not only are they dumb beasts that God has given us to care for, but they're Miss Finlayson's pets too. Now, I want you to go and knock on her door and tell her what you've done to her cats, and apologize to her for hurting them. Then on Sunday, you're to offer up those tuppence to God on the offering plate, or I'll bring you up before the elders."

"Y-yes sir," chorused Rory and James. Their two dark heads nodded in frightened agreement and their eyes were large with apprehension.

"Go then, and make your apologies to Miss Finlayson." The two boys disappeared into the gathering dusk. Presently Angus heard them rap on Catherine's door. After a moment the glow from a candle lit the door space and he could hear the sound of their young voices confessing their current sin to Catherine.

Chapter 6

Angus stood in the darkness just beyond the reach of the candle light. Tears hovered on the edges of the children's voices as they made their confessions.

"And are you sorry that you did this?" he heard Catherine ask. She leaned her stout body toward the boys and peered nearsightedly out at them.

"Y-yes, Miss Finlayson," they chorused and backed slightly away from her.

"You'll never do such a thing as this again?"

"N-no, Miss Finlayson." The quaver in their voices was more noticeable now. "And did you hurt them?" Concern for her pets roughened her voice and it seemed to rumble from somewhere deep in her chest.

"Their tails were pinched but they were still able to run," said James.

"My poor pussies! It was a bad thing you did, but you're sorry for it and you know now that it was wrong to treat an animal so. Come in then, and we'll have a cup of tea and get better acquainted." She ushered the boys into her kitchen. "The cats'll be back in the morning, I have no doubt, but they'll just never trust a boy again." The door closed softly on the gathering darkness.

Angus smiled to himself. Catherine's a good soul, he thought. He turned to continue his walk toward the manse, his mind busy with the events of the evening. I just cannot understand what's taken young Donald these days. He's not himself at all. Poor Ian has his hands full with him. This latest escapade was just plain cruel. His mother'd be ashamed of him. Angus shook his head. I don't know if I should tell Ian about this or not. It would only be adding to his burden. I'll see what Mary'll say, she's got good sense.

Lamplight glowed from the home of the minister. Angus strode down the short lane. In the darkness ahead a shadowy figure loomed. Angus checked his pace and squinted into the thick darkness. The shadow became one with the spruce tree beside the house. Angus moved carefully forward, his eyes strained wide, his ears tuned for any sound.

"Is that you Angus?" The shadow detached itself from the spruce tree and came to meet him.

"Aye, it's me," replied Angus. "Is that you, William?"

"It's me. You scared the liver out of me, walking so close behind me like that and never identifying yourself."

"I didn't see you until just now, nor hear you either."

"Well, you've been following me ever since Catherine's. I thought the *bocans* were after me."

"I came out of Catherine's. I caught Little Rory and James tying up her cats."

"Is that what all the racket was about? It sounded right eerie from the track."

"I guess it would, they were howling right enough. Why didn't you call out to me?"

"You were only a shadow passing in and out of other shadows and I was that afraid. All I could think of was that the murderer was abroad again. You're all wrapped in your coat so I couldn't see the shape of you. I thought I was done for."

Another shape materialized out of the shadows of the lane.

"G'd'evening, Sam."

A chirp of fright escaped Sam's lips and he began to run. In a moment he had gained the safety of the minister's house and closed the door behind himself without waiting to be invited.

"It's a terrible thing what this has done to us," said Angus.

"Aye, and it'll be a long day before the effects of it are finished."

The two men walked on to the house together. Angus rapped on the door.

"G'd'evening, Angus, William. Come right in. Hang your coats behind the stove so they'll be warm for when you leave." Mrs. MacDonald bustled around getting extra chairs and pouring out cups of tea to warm cold hands.

"This meeting will come to order." Lochie rapped on the kitchen table with his knuckles. Sam, as secretary, scribbled in his notebook. Minutes were read and approved. Old business was followed up and new business was begun.

"The squirrels have found their way into the church attic," said Mr. MacDonald. "I was up there after some papers last week and I found their handiwork."

"Indeed," said William, "we'll have to get at that right away before we have a leak. It'd be a terrible shame if the water came in on that beautiful ceiling."

"Aye, it's a work of art in itself," agreed Sam. "All that intricate woodwork, it's irreplaceable, especially now since John the Joiner died."

"He was, indeed, a craftsman," said David, "and there's no one to replace him."

"I don't suppose you can do that kind of work, can you?" asked Lochie. "Your father was awful good with that sort of thing."

"Not me," said David, "I'm only a rough sort of carpenter. Teaching school's my only real skill."

"I can fix the roof," offered Angus. "I have some shingles left over from doing the barn roof the other year. They'll be just the ticket."

"It's settled then," said Lochie. "Angus'll repair the church roof at his earliest convenience."

"It's time to bank the church again," said John the Store. "I noticed quite a draft around my feet last Sunday."

"Yes, can we get together sometime this week and do

that?" asked Lochie.

"I can come on Thursday," said Sam. "I was planning to do my own house this week."

"Can anyone else come on Thursday?" asked Lochie.

"Thursday afternoon's fine with me," said Angus. Heads nodded in agreement around the kitchen.

"We should put up the storm windows then, too."

"The graveyard needs tidying too, before the snow comes."

"The ladies usually look after that," said Lochie. "We'll leave it to them."

The business concluded and Mrs. MacDonald passed tea and buttered bread and cheese. "Just a wee *strupach* to keep you on your way home. It's a cold dark night."

"I'll walk with you and William," said Sam. He swallowed the last of his tea and mopped at his moustache with an immaculate handkerchief. I'd be obliged if one or the other of you would walk to my lane with me, too. I had a terrible fright coming over. Someone called my name right out of the darkness."

"Where was that?" asked William.

"In this very lane. I had all I could do to keep from

crying out."

"That was only us," said Angus. "William and I had just scared the daylights out of each other. We didn't mean to frighten you, too, but you left so fast we didn't have a chance to come forward."

"Nevertheless," said Sam, "I will accompany you on the way home."

Angus trudged toward home after accompanying Sam to his own gate. The moon had risen and the countryside around was a shifting panorama of shadow and light. Presently he reached his own gate and stood for a moment gazing across the fields that were his farm. *It's a shame that this land'll likely grow up in trees when we're gone. I regret not having a son. I have no one to leave my property to, and the fields that I stopped farming two years ago are already going back to woods. I had thought to leave it to young Donald, him being my closest relative after Ian, but I don't know anymore, the way he's behaving.* The gate clicked shut behind him and he started down the lane, his pace quickening as he caught sight of the soft glow of candle light from his kitchen windows. He could picture Mary there, darning a sock or hemming a winter shirt for him and humming one of the old songs, and he felt warmed by it. He slipped quietly into the candle-shadowy kitchen and stood for a moment watching her work. She sensed his presence and looked up from her mending, and smiled.

"You're home, then," she said with satisfaction.

He pulled a chair closer to the fire and sat down.

"Did you have a good meeting?"

"Aye, everyone was there. We did some planning for the church. It needs repairs before the snow flies."

"Nothing big, I hope."

"No, it's just a bunch of little things. The roof needs inspection, the squirrels have been up there and it looks like they might have caused some damage that'll need repair before it causes a leak. I said I'd go up tomorrow and see to it." He fell silent, staring into the little flame that still leapt and danced from the embers of their suppertime fire.

Mary looked at him keenly. "What's troubling you, then?"

Angus met her bright gaze. "I was just thinking about all the unhappiness that Anna's death has caused us, and we're no nearer to finding out who did it than the day it was done."

"Did you see Ian this evening?" Mary picked up her work again.

"No, but I saw the work of Donald, and it wasn't good." The chair squeaked as Angus shifted his position. "D'you know that young rascal paid Little Rory and James tuppence each to tie up Catherine's cats together by the tails and hang them over the clothesline?" Indignation filled his voice. "The poor beasts were that frantic by the time I got there to free them! They'll never be the same again."

"Oh, dear-o! And she always made such pets of them. They were like her children. She'd have them in the house and everything. She'll be heartbroken if they were hurt."

"Well, I fixed the two young imps that did it. They're not even going to profit from their mischief. I made them go and tell Catherine what they'd done and they're to put the tuppence onto the collection plate next Sunday or face the elders." Angus laughed. "But it's not the elders they have to worry about. When their mother and father find out about the money that they can't explain …" He left the rest unsaid.

"I wonder where Donald got four pence to give away? I didn't know Ian paid him."

"Well, that's just it, where did he get the money? I'm wondering myself if I should tell Ian about this. He's got enough to contend with now. What d'you think, Mary?"

Mary considered this in silence for a few moments, her hands idle in her lap. "It's true enough that he's got his hands full, but he can't remedy the situation without all the facts. I don't think it would be a kindness to keep this from him. It may be something that needs nipping in the bud. Donald may be heading for some real trouble that perhaps could be prevented if his father knew." She took up her mending again, and settled her glasses more firmly on the end of her nose.

Angus looked across at her as she bent her grey head to her task, her work-roughened hands always so capable, neatly hemming a patch on his trousers that would make them serve another year. A great love for his wife filled his heart and he leaned over and kissed her wrinkled cheek, a rare expression of caring from an undemonstrative man. "You're a good and wise woman, Mary," he said.

She smiled back at him. "And I'm married to a good man."

Anna's Secret

❖

The next morning dawned as bright as the day before, but there were clouds to the west and the smell of rain was faint on the autumn air.

Angus stood in his barn doorway and sniffed the salt-fresh breeze from the Strait. There'll be rain before night, he thought. I'd better go today and see to the church roof. The sooner the better perhaps.

He turned and disappeared into the dimness of the barn. "Move over, Bossy!" He shouldered the cow to the side of her stall to make room for himself and the milking stool. He settled himself on the stool with the bucket between his knees and began the rhythmical job of milking. Presently he began to sing. "We hail with joy the dawning morn …" He cleared his throat and tried a lower pitch. "We hail with joy the approaching day …" His voice wobbled on around the melody. He cleared his throat again. "Well, Bossy, I'll never make a precentor. I don't know how William does it. He always seems to hit just the right note for everyone to sing, even old Bessie with all her fancy Charlottetown voice training and her high C's." He cleared his throat once more, struck another pitch and found one to his liking.

His hands took up the rhythm of the hymn. The cow let down the richness of her milk as he sang, and peace filled the barn. By the fifteenth verse the task was nearly finished, the bucket filled brim full with foaming milk, warm and sweet from the cow. Angus set the full bucket aside and picked up the cats' dish

"Come, Pussies," he called as he stripped the last of the milk from the cow into the old bent pan that was their dish. The three cats who kept the barn almost free of mice appeared out of the darkness of the hayloft.

"Well, mother, you must have had your kittens," said Angus addressing the old black cat. "Where'd you hide them this time? Not too deep in the hay, I hope. You know I'm not as young as I used to be, and I can't be climbing all through the hay looking for your offspring."

The cat looked at him enquiringly. "Merow?"

"You heard me," said Angus as he untied the cow and opened the gate to the pasture. "Perhaps I'll wait until you bring them out. Catherine might be wanting a couple of kittens if her two don't come back." He picked up the bucket of milk and carried it to the house.

"It looks like rain, Mary. I think I might just go over and take a look at the church roof this morning. Better to be safe than sorry. A good downpour of rain would be the ruination of all the ceilings."

"And the floors too, no doubt," said Mary. "I'd go with you and visit with Rachael, but I must set bread this morning or we'll not have a bite for the Sabbath."

"Well, I won't be long, anyway." Angus closed the door behind him. He collected some spare shingles from the shop, filled his pockets with a handful of nails, and picked up his hammer. I hope there's a ladder there, he thought. I don't want to have to lug one from Lochie's. He set out on the path toward the church.

The morning sky was losing its blue brightness as the clouds moved in from the west. The air was damper now. Angus quickened his step. I'll have to hurry if I don't want to get wet, he thought and picked up his pace. Ahead in the distance he could see a sturdy figure coming toward him. Presently they met.

"G'day, Donald," said Angus. "You're not in school today?"

Donald ducked his head. "No, sir, Poppa wanted me to help him in the big barn today."

"I see. So you're on an errand for him now, are you?"

"Yes, sir." Donald's reply was very brief.

"Well, I'm off to see to the church roof and the rain is on its way, so I'd better hurry. Greet your father for me, and g'day to you." He nodded to Donald and hurried on.

I didn't think Ian had any repairs to do in the big barn, thought Angus as he strode away from Donald. Ah, well, he might've and just never mentioned it. It seems a strange thing though, that he'd keep Donald out of school just for that, with him and Anna so intent on Donald getting a good education.

Angus walked around the church surveying the steep roof for damage. Well, wouldn't you know! I'll have to go to the peak and there's not a ladder in sight. He turned toward Lochie's and was soon back with his ladder.

I hope I brought enough shingles, I see there's another one or two loose on the eaves. Maybe a nail will do the trick. He settled the ladder against the edge of the roof and began to climb. I think the next time this roof needs repair someone else'll have to do it. My knees aren't what they used to be. He scrambled to the peak of the roof to inspect the damage. *I don't think this was squirrels, more likely the wind away up here.* He straddled the peak and pulled away the damaged shingles and began nailing the new ones into place. *We're going to need a new roof soon if this's any indication.* A drop of rain struck his cheek. His hammer pounded faster. *There, that'll have to do for now.* He turned and began a careful slide down the roof just in time to see his ladder wobble and move away from the eaves.

"Here, now!" he shouted, "don't go away with my ladder. How'm I to get down from here?"

No one answered and the ladder was not returned. The sound of footsteps on the quiet grass was barely discernible.

"Now who would do such a thing?" muttered Angus as another drop of cold rain struck his face. "I'll catch my death of pneumonia up here without even a coat to cover me, and dear knows how long it'll be before anyone comes this way again." The rain began to pour in earnest. "Well, whoever you were I hope you get as good and wet as I'll be." He scurried to the small shelter of the steeple and crouched there out of the worst of the wind and wet.

The downpour was brief and the pounding rain soon eased to a heavy drizzle. Angus edged out from behind his shelter and shivered as the dampness found its way through his final layer of clothing. *It'll be a fine thing if I slip on this wet roof,* he thought as he began a controlled slide down to the eaves. *Poor Mary'll be a widow before her time.* He peered over the edge of the roof. The ladder was nowhere in sight. Angus worked his way to the far end and peered over again. "Drat! Whoever took it must have hidden it," he muttered, "not that it'd do me much good lying on the ground." He scrambled up to the peak and slid carefully down the other side. He sneezed, then shivered, then sneezed again. *I'll catch my death of cold up here,* he thought as he pulled his rain-damp handkerchief from his pocket and blew his nose loudly.

"Angus, is that you up there?" a voice called from the other side of the church.

"Aye, it's me alright, and I'm catching my death of pneumonia," he replied and scrambled over the peak once more. He peered over the edge of the roof. There was no one there. *I'm hearing things already. It's worse than I thought.*

Anna's Secret

"Where are you?" The voice came again, this time from the other side of the roof.

Angus recognized the voice this time. "I'm over here," he replied.

"Well, stay where you are, then," came the voice again.

Presently Duncan's sturdy frame came around the end of the building. He was closely followed by Hector.

"What're you doing up there in this rain, Angus? You'll catch your death of cold, and then what'll Mary do?" The two brothers stood staring up at Angus.

"How'd you get up there without a ladder?" asked Duncan.

"I flew!" Angus' patience was wearing thin. "Now'll you go and get a ladder so I can get down again."

Hector blinked. "Well, if you flew up, why can't you fly down again?" He turned the problem over in his mind. The process was nearly visible.

"Oh, never mind. Just go and get a ladder. Lochie has one if the thief hasn't stolen it altogether." Angus sneezed again.

Hector turned to look at Duncan. "Maybe it was the *bocans* that stole his ladder in the first place."

"If it was, they've hidden it well," replied Duncan. "Are you sure you had a ladder?" he called up to Angus.

"Just go and get a ladder," said Angus. "It's starting to rain again and I'm already soaked." Another fit of sneezing began. "Will you two hurry." He gasped and blew his nose once more as the drizzle changed rapidly to another heavy downpour. He scrambled up the roof again and took what shelter he could behind the steeple.

Duncan and Hector ambled off in the direction of Alexander's arguing all the way. The rain had almost ceased when they returned.

"Where'd you two go anyway?" asked Angus when he reached the ground. "I thought you were going to Lochie's for his ladder. Whose is this?"

"Alexander's," replied Duncan.

"But Alexander's is three miles in the other direction and Lochie's is just next door," said Angus.

"Well, you said yourself that it was Lochie's ladder that you had in the first place and someone took it. Why would we go to Lochie's looking for a ladder that we knew he didn't have?"

Angus groaned. "Oh, never mind." He turned and

walked briskly toward Lochie's. Hector and Duncan followed him at a trot.

"You needn't walk so fast." complained Hector, panting a little as he tried to keep up to Angus' stride.

"Lochie's not going to move in the next five minutes," said Duncan. "That is where you're going, isn't it?"

Angus sneezed in reply. "It's the nearest place to get a hot cup of tea." He hurried on.

"Who d'you think took the ladder?" Hector drew abreast of Angus.

"I don't know," said Angus, "but I'm going to find out." He crossed Lochie's rain-soaked barnyard almost at a run, the wet mud greasy beneath his feet. "I believe you gentlemen were on your way somewhere else?" he said.

"Och, we were only going to the store for some tobacco," said Duncan, "but that can wait."

"Well, I'm not sure it can. John was nearly out of it when I was there earlier," said Angus. "His new shipment hasn't arrived yet and he doesn't know when it'll be in. It'd be a shame if you had to go without for lack of foresight."

Hector and Duncan looked at one another torn between the need to know and the need for tobacco.

"We have enough to last us until tomorrow if we're careful," said Hector.

"I'll tell you about it when I see you again," said Angus.

"Promise?" asked Duncan.

"I'll do what I can." Angus knocked on Lochie's door. "You'd better hurry."

"Yes, indeed, we'd better hurry. We'll be that distressed if it doesn't come in until next week." They hurried off just as Lochie opened the door.

"What in the world happened to you?" asked Lochie.

"Someone took my ladder and left me on the church roof, I'm soaked through."

"Come in and get dry then." Lochie stood aside to allow Angus to enter the kitchen. "Rachael's gone to visit her sister in Lyndale for the day." He stoked up the fire and pulled the kettle closer to the heat. "I thought you returned the ladder an hour ago."

"It wasn't me;" replied Angus, "but I'd like to know who it was."

"Well, I thought you were awful quick about your work. The rain came so fast after you left I thought maybe you'd abandoned the idea after all and just put the ladder back."

Angus shook his head. "No, I was hurrying to get it done. I was almost finished when the rain started. I drove a couple of more nails just to be sure, and when I turned around I saw the ladder being taken away. I couldn't get down from the peak fast enough to see who did it and the rain came down so hard after that, all I could do was try to shelter myself behind the steeple."

"Well, get yourself out of that wet shirt and I'll get you a dry one to put on. You may not be able to button it, but at least it'll keep your back warm until this one dries." Lochie disappeared into the tiny bedroom off the kitchen. Presently he returned with a dry shirt and handed it to Angus. "This one's the biggest I could find."

Angus hung his wet shirt on the hook behind the stove and struggled into Lochie's old shirt.

"Maybe I should have brought a blanket instead." He went back into the little bedroom and stripped the blanket off the bed. "Rachael'll just have to fix it when she gets home." He handed the blanket to Angus.

"You didn't notice anything about the person who returned the ladder, did you?" Angus wrapped himself in the coverlet and pulled his chair closer to the fire.

"No, just that he resembled you in stature." Lochie filled the teapot and spooned in a generous portion of leaves shaved from the block of tea. "That's why I thought it was you."

"Hm," said Angus. "That could have been any one of several people. I'm not the only one who's short and stocky around here."

"Was there anyone else about when you went to the church?"

"I met young Donald on an errand for his father on my way here," said Angus, "but he wouldn't do such a thing. His father'd skin him."

"What was Donald doing out of school? I thought the schoolmaster had them preparing for the fall concert today."

"Well, I didn't hear about that. All I know is that Donald said his father had work for him to do and he stayed home." Angus hitched his chair still closer to the fire and sneezed. "And why would he do such a thing anyway?"

"I don't know, but my Neil says that Donald's been awful queer since his mother died. He won't hang around with the other boys at all now." Lochie got up and went to the pantry.

"Aye, well, he's taken it awful hard. T'was a bad time in his life for such a thing to have happened. He was still a child in so many ways, and a boy needs his mother."

"Will you have a cookie with your tea?" Lochie called from the dimness of the cubby hole across the room.

"That would be right welcome," said Angus as Lochie emerged from the pantry carrying two thick mugs. "Rachael makes some of the best cookies around."

Chapter 7

"I'm glad that cold didn't develop into anything." Mary folded the last of the towels and put them away. "It'd be a terrible burden on someone's conscience if you'd taken pneumonia and died." Her face took on a worried look as she stood staring blankly into the warming cupboard behind the stove. "I don't know what I'd do without you, and all for a cruel prank."

"Now, Mary." Angus put his arm around her shoulder. "There's no use thinking about what might have happened. The fact is that it didn't, and it was your excellent nursing that prevented it."

"Humph! My nursing! A lot of good it would have done if you'd had anything more than a cold." She turned herself impatiently out of his arm. "You're a young man yet, and what am I supposed to do if you're taken, and all because of someone else's foolishness?"

"I'm not so young anymore. It was all I could do to climb to the peak of the church the other day. I'm past fifty and so are you. It won't be too many years before one of us is taken."

"Well, I hope the Lord will spare us for a while yet."

"The Lord giveth and the Lord taketh away. Just look at poor Anna."

"That was none of the Lord's doing, and you know it. That was the work of the devil, if ever I saw it."

"Well now, whoever did it is getting away with it quite handily. Man or devil, he's managed to cover his tracks without a trace."

"It'll never be solved now, not likely." Tears roughened Mary's voice and she cleared her throat. "Poor Anna. Her life taken in such a way and none of us able to help her." Mary turned away, unable to hide the tear that had escaped her vigilance. "The ragged ends of this evil deed will haunt us for a long time to come." She rummaged in her apron pocket for a handkerchief, then blew her nose noisily.

"Perhaps you're worried about Anna returning to haunt us," teased Angus in an awkward attempt to lighten the moment.

"She'd never do such a thing." Mary's grief turned to anger in an instant. "Anna was always concerned about others. It won't matter to her now who killed her." Her blue eyes flashed a warning. "Anna was one of the best. She was my friend."

"Aye, and friend to a lot of others," said Angus, now eager to placate Mary's wrath.

"We'd all do well to remember it."

"You finish chores," said Ian after the milking was done. "I must go to a meeting at the church, and I'm late as it is."

Donald shrugged and kept on working.

"I'll not be late. Don't forget to skim the milk and wash out the buckets."

Donald didn't reply.

Ian turned away. He's so sullen these days I don't know how to approach him. Ian reviewed the events of the last few months as he hurried into the porch and poured a dipperful of water into the battered tin wash pan. I wonder if I should trim my beard, he thought. I haven't done it lately. He regarded himself in the watery mirror and rubbed his hand across his face. I don't have time if I'm to meet Angus. He dipped his hands into the cool water and rubbed a little soap on them. Clean will have to do. We'll soon be out of soap. Anna was just about ready to make soap when she died.

His heart seemed to turn over in his chest at the sudden memory of Anna tending the soap kettle in the yard, her auburn hair, made a little untidy by the wind and the heat of the task, shining in the sunlight, her strong body bent and turned as she wielded the paddle. He remembered his surprise that she knew how to make soap when he married her. She seemed so young to know the things she knew. I thought I was marrying a child and it was a woman I married. The knot of pain in his heart seemed to tighten. He turned and scrubbed vigorously at his face with the rough towel to banish the tightness. He forced his mind on to practical things. I wonder would Mary make me some soap when she's making her own if I gave her the fat Anna'd been saving. He buttoned on a clean shirt, the wrinkles in it a testament to his ineptitude with the smoothing iron.

At last he was striding up the hill and was soon passing the place where so few months ago Anna had lain in such stillness. He hurried past the spot and did not look at it. He shivered. A hint of night cold was already on the breeze. Somewhere an owl hooted and the rustle of small animals sounded softly in the stubble of the hay field. A twig cracked in Old Rory's wood. Ian's heart raced then slowed. It's nothing, he comforted himself. He looked in the direction of the woods. The rustle of leaves ceased and a faint glow seemed to disappear as Ian turned his head to look directly at it. His heart raced again. He looked straight ahead and strode on even faster. He looked out the corner of his eye. The glow seemed to be still there but when he looked at it directly, it disappeared. He hurried on until his shins began to hurt and he was forced to slow his pace. I'll walk backwards for a bit. He turned around. The glow that wasn't there turned with him and seemed to hover over the path he had just traversed. He stopped his backward pace and stood, frozen there by his imagination. The light continued on toward him. Rough voices sounded on the night air but in his fear Ian was unable to take them in.

"It's the *bocans*," he whispered. "They've come to get

me." His feet seemed glued to the ground and he was unable to turn and run. He stared at the advancing light, his eyelids strained stiffly open. The faint voices grew louder as the light grew larger. Ian's hearing began to work again, and the voices resolved themselves into the sound of human neighbours

"Is that you, Ian?" Duncan swung his lantern as he walked making the shadows bob and twist, sometimes near and sometimes farther away.

Ian cleared his throat. "Aye, it's me." Relief made his voice sound faint and far away in his own ears.

"What's the matter with you? asked Hector. "You're as white as a sheet." He peered into Ian's face.

"You startled me, that's all. All I could see was your light following me. I didn't know what it was. I saw it first over by Old Rory's wood and thought it was a strange place for a light since there's not much over there." He turned on his heel and marched on down the path.

Hector and Duncan looked at each other then hurried after Ian. "Indeed it is a strange place for our light to be since we weren't over there." Duncan puffed a little in his effort to keep up with Ian's urgent stride.

"Maybe it was one of those optical illusions." Ian lengthened his stride in a vain effort to out-distance Hector and Duncan.

"What's an optical illusion?" asked Hector.

"It's when you see something that isn't there," replied Ian.

"D'you mean like the *bocans*?"

"Something like that." Ian saw his chance to get rid of their company and took it. "There's no such thing as the *bocans*." Duncan held his lantern a little higher.

"There is so," Hector insisted. "I saw one once over by Old Annie's."

"That must have been awhile ago," said Ian. "Old Annie hasn't lived by herself for at least ten years now."

"Oh, it was, it was." Hector nodded hard. "I was just a lad. I was passing her house on a night just like this one and out of the woods came a black cat. It was a big one. It wound around my legs as if it wanted to trip me. I kicked at it and it ran away. It ran back to the woods and turned into a ball of light and floated into the trees. It was just about then that the owl hooted and I took to my heels, and I never looked back."

"It's probably just as well," said Duncan, "for you

wouldn't have wanted to see Old Annie standing in her doorway laughing at you. It was probably her you heard hooting."

"Humph! A lot you know about it. You weren't even there."

Ian turned into Angus' lane. "I'll see you gentlemen another day."

"Are you leaving us?" asked Duncan.

"I have a meeting at the church and Angus is going with me."

"We'll wait then, and walk with you," said Hector.

"If you wish."

Just then an owl hooted nearby. It sounded large and threatening. Hector and Duncan exchanged nervous glances.

"I think we'll just keep walking," said Duncan. "You and Angus can catch up to us. We won't have gotten far." They turned as a unit and hurried down the track, Duncan's lantern casting weird shadows and lights into the grass of the ditches.

They'll be half way to Charlottetown before they stop, thought Ian. He quickened his pace now that the path had returned to its dark silence. A twig snapped under his foot and Angus' dog began to bark.

"Quiet! Be quiet lad! It's only Ian." It was Angus' voice. The dog stopped barking and began sniffing around Ian's feet. '"Evening, Angus. Are you ready to go?"

"Aye, I've been waiting these past five minutes."

"Only five minutes. I thought I was later than that. I must have made better time than I thought."

"Well, with the company you keep, I'm not surprised. Did you like my imitation of an owl?"

"Was that you, then?"

"It was me, though I'm having a twinge of conscience over it now."

"Och, it won't hurt them to take a long walk this evening, it's a nice evening for it."

Angus laughed. "Aye, they have their lantern to keep the *bocans* away."

They walked on in companionable silence for a few minutes.

Presently Ian said, "I hear you had a bad cold."

"I did, and it was through no fault of my own."

"They never are, they seem to have a mind all their own."

"No, I mean I wouldn't have had one at all if someone

hadn't stolen my ladder when I was up fixing the church roof. Whoever it was left me there in that rainstorm the other day and I got a good soaking." A residue of anger still sounded in Angus' voice.

"Who would do such a thing?"

"Who knows? Someone with an evil sense of humour I suppose." They trudged on in silence for a few yards.

"I ran into your Donald over by Lochie's the other day. He said he was on an errand for you instead of being in school."

"On a school day? Certainly not! I'll have a word with him when I get home."

"Well now, I don't want to be making trouble for the boy. I just thought you should know about it, that's all."

Ian sighed. "He's in more trouble than that. I have a veritable list of deeds that need explaining."

"Oh?" said Angus.

"Aye, I found Anna's money jar out of its place the other day. I don't know how much was in it so I don't know how much was taken. Maybe there was none taken, but it shouldn't have been out." The sadness was back in Ian's voice. "She was saving to send him to college."

"There was at least four pence taken. I found the use it was put to the other evening."

"And what was that? Mischief, no doubt."

"Aye, it was mischief all right. He paid Little Rory and young James to tie up Catherine's cats by the tails and hang them over the clothesline. It was a frightful racket. I caught them at it and set the cats free. I don't think they'll ever be the same again."

"The cats or the boys?" A glimmer of laughter ran through Ian's voice again.

"Either one. I put the fear into the boys about sin and made them go and apologize to Catherine. They were to put the pennies in the offering plate on Sunday. I don't know if the cats came back or not."

"So that's where the extra money came from on Sunday."

"That's where. And that's why Rory and James were being marched home by the ears after church. Their mothers were just savage. I don't think they'll live this one down for awhile."

"Aye, and Catherine'll have more cats than she knows what to do with once the word gets out that her pussies are missing."

Ian opened his eyes to the watery light of an overcast dawn. He stretched and yawned, his mind not yet focused on the events of yesterday. In the next room Donald stirred and grunted, and the memory of his conversation with Angus came rushing back. It lay like a weight on his chest and he groaned with the heaviness of it.

What am I to do with Donald? He's getting out of hand. I can't imagine what he could have been thinking of, torturing animals, and getting the little boys to do the deed for him. He should be ashamed! Ian rolled out of bed, his bare feet cringing at the cold of the autumn floor. A frost last night, and it's barely October.

The window pane had a necklace of frost that was just now beginning to melt with the encroaching day. Ian pulled on his chilly clothing and hurried downstairs calling out to Donald as he went. "Wake up, Donald, there's work to be done." Another grunt issued forth from Donald's room.

Soon the sounds of early morning activities filled the house. An armload of wood rumbled into the wood box The stove lid clanked as Ian lifted it to inspect what was left of last night's fire. "Stone cold," he grumbled as he sifted through the ashes searching for an ember or two. Kindling crackled as Ian sliced thin strips of wood lengthwise off the larger piece with the old kitchen knife. The snap of a match and presently the fire was warming the small kitchen and the smell of wood smoke filled the air. The kettle began to sing on the stove, and the porridge bubbled and talked to itself in the pot.

"Donald!" Ian bellowed from the bottom of the steep stairs. "It's time!"

Ian set two bowls and spoons, and two thick china mugs on the table. Presently Donald arrived in the kitchen.

"I hear you were up to no good the other evening," said Ian.

A closed look came down on Donald's face. "What do you mean?"

"What had you to do with the torture of Miss Finlayson's cats?"

"Nothing." Donald's reply was almost rude.

"I understand you were smart enough to get children to do your work for you. 'Whosoever shall offend one of these little ones that believe in me, it is better for him that a millstone were hanged about his neck, and he were cast into the sea.' How could you do such a thing? Causing those children to do wrong." Ian paused for breath, then remembered the next item on the list. "And where'd you get the money for it?"

Donald shrugged and started to get up from his place at the table.

"Sit down!" roared Ian. "I know where you got the money. I saw your tracks. It was your mother's money that she was saving for your education, and that's nothing short of stealing."

"Well, it was to be mine anyway."

"Not until one of us gave it to you. How much did you take?"

"Just four pence."

"And how do you plan to return it?"

Donald shrugged. "I don't want to go to college anyway."

"Your mother wanted you to and you'll go whether you want to or not, which brings me to my other point. Why weren't you in school the other day?"

"Didn't want to be." Donald stared at his cooling porridge.

"And what did you do with yourself all day? And where did you go?"

"Nothing. Nowhere."

"Be sure your sins'll find you out. If you don't tell me, I'll hear about it soon enough."

Donald shrugged again and continued to stare at his plate.

"Will you stop that damn shrugging." Ian's tirade stopped as the shame of having cursed at his son flooded over him. His apology came swiftly. "I'm sorry son. That was wrong of me to have spoken to you so."

Donald grunted and left the table, the remainder of his porridge still cooling in its bowl.

Ian looked after him as the door slammed behind him. "Oh, Donald, what am I to do for you? Lying and stealing and leading little children astray, and playing truant. Whatever can I do for you?" He rose to clear the table. "But my heart is heaviest for having cursed at you."

An awkward peace held between Ian and Donald for the next few days. Ian tried to bridge the gap but all he was able to elicit from Donald were monosyllables and grunts.

"I'm going to take the barrel of fat over to Mary this afternoon. She said she'd be making soap next week and would make ours at the same time. I want you to kill the old brown hen this morning and I'll take that with me.

They'll enjoy a chicken dinner on Sunday. I'm going to pull the last of the turnips this morning. I'll take one of those too."

Ian drained the last of the tea from his mug and set it in the pantry. I'll have to get at these dishes soon. Anna'd be so ashamed at the look of her pantry these days. He hurried out of doors. Presently he heard the sound of the axe and the noisy squawk of a hen in distress. At least he's doing as he's told for once, he thought as he picked up his hoe and set it in the wheelbarrow. Perhaps he's over his fit of behaviour now.

A short time later Ian observed Donald heading schoolward with his books and slate under his arm. He felt a sudden relaxing somewhere in the region of his heart. He'll do all right, he thought, happy for the first time in months. He straightened his shoulders and returned to his hoeing with new energy.

The day remained cool and grey. At a distance, haze hid the woods. Except for the crows, even the birds were silent. A few hours later Ian had stored the last of the turnips in the red clay darkness of the cellar. He knocked the moist clinging earth off the hoe and leaned it against the barn wall to dry. There's lots of turnip greens. We'll have some tonight with our supper. Mary'll probably be glad for a few. He gathered some into a bucket. Catherine'll probably like some too. He added more greens to the bucket. I'll bring her a little turnip to go with them, she's right on the way, and I know she can't keep a garden anymore with her rheumatism.

Ian went about his tasks with a light heart. It feels good to think of others instead of myself for a change. Soon he had the wheelbarrow loaded with the keg of fat and the bucket of greens. I'll just go and get the hen now, she should be well drained.

He stepped into the cool dimness of the wood house His eyes slowly adjusted to the lack of light. He blinked and saw the hen hanging from the rafter at the back with the bucket below her to catch the blood. He pulled out his pocket knife to cut the string that held her but it slipped from his grasp. Drat! He bent to pick it up. He leaned on the edge of the chopping block to balance himself and recoiled at the sight before him. The hen's head lay in neat slivers from the beak to the neck, her yellow eye stared blankly back at him from the centre of one of the slices.

Ian swallowed hard as the bile rose in his throat. So that's what all the noise was about this morning. The tears of frustration felt hot and strange as they struggled for release from his eyes. He blinked them back and the heavy weight returned to his chest. He carried the chopping block outdoors and scraped the remains of the hen off into the soft clay of the turnip field. "At least you could have hidden your handiwork," he muttered, "and not leave it for others to find."

Ian's heart was heavy as he picked up the handles of the wheelbarrow and headed toward Angus' house; the horror of his find in the woodshed was still fresh in his mind. *I suppose the hen'll be as tough as shoe leather and not fit to eat. Such a waste of good food.* The path steepened and he grunted with the increased effort required to push the wheelbarrow. *He's too big to thrash or he'd feel the broad end of the strap.* Ian remembered with surprise the breadth of his son's shoulders as he had sat hunched at the breakfast table that morning. *He's as big as I am now. I couldn't thrash him if I tried.* A sense of great helplessness came over him and he stopped for breath. He wiped his streaming forehead with the sleeve of his shirt. *This hill is* steeper than I thought. He stood looking at the slope ahead of him for a moment longer then turned the wheelbarrow and positioning himself between the handles, began the long pull up the hill.

The sound of Angus' axe echoed off the buildings of his farm. The axe sliced through a piece of birch with a single stroke of his strong arms. The work ceased when Dog announced Ian's arrival. In the apple orchard Mary was taking clothes off the line, the pile of snowy shirts and sheets nearly hiding her from view.

"G'day, Angus." Ian set down his load and inspected his calloused hands for blisters.

"G'day, Ian, you look warm." Angus rested his hands on the end of the axe handle for a moment.

"It's a long walk with such a heavy load." Ian sat down on the tree stump beside the woodpile where Angus was working. "Mary said she'd make me some soap when she was making yours if I brought over the fat that Anna'd been saving. I pulled the last of the turnip this morning and I brought you over a nice one and some greens."

"A plump hen, too, I see. That'll make a good dinner

on Sunday and leftovers until Wednesday. You'll have to come and join us after church. Yourself and Donald, if he'll come."

"You may not be able to eat the hen, and Donald doesn't deserve to come."

"Why? What's he done now?" Angus set down his axe and sat down on top of the chopping block.

"It was a terrible thing he did today. The worst yet." Ian sighed a monumental sigh. "He deserves a thrashing for it but he's too big now."

"Thrashing never did anyone much good anyway. It only makes him resentful and more apt to do worse than before." He waited for Ian to continue.

Ian sighed again. The weight in his chest seemed larger than ever. "Anna'd be so ashamed of him. She'd never have condoned harming innocent animals."

"Has he been after Catherine's cats again?"

"Worse. He beheaded that poor hen in the wheelbarrow there in slices. I found the results of his evil work after he'd gone off to school." Ian got up from his stump and began to pace. "The hen may be too tough to eat, and what am I going to do about this trick?"

"Don't worry about the hen, Mary can stew her. I don't know what you can do about Donald. I truly don't. I suppose he'll grow out of it in time. It seems a shame that he was so attached to Anna that he can't mourn properly and recover from it like the rest of us."

"I used to worry about the closeness that he and Anna had when he was a little fellow. I told her that she'd be turning him into a weakling." Ian stopped pacing and looked at Angus. "She just laughed and said it wouldn't happen, and after that she'd send him out to work with me at whatever I was doing and the attachment seemed to right itself." Ian lapsed into silence for a few minutes.

"But there were still things I didn't know about. I was too worried about her traipsing off to see James I wasn't paying attention. It seemed like she'd go two or three times a week, and there was not a thing I could do to stop her."

"Aye, well you had your hands full, but it's all water under the bridge now. It's time to forget about the unpleasantness and uncertainties and remember Anna for her goodnesses. She was very kind, you know."

"She was that. I never had to have a thought about the running of the house or the garden when she was alive, and if she thought I would be needing something about the farm she'd be there with it even before I could think of it myself." Ian rested his elbows on his knees. "I just never understood her fixation with James."

"Nor did anyone else. I thought she had dropped all thoughts of him when she married you and he went away."

"So did I. She seemed happy enough. She didn't seem to pine after him even when he was first gone. She didn't even seem particularly excited when he returned."

"Have you been by James' since that last time you were there?"

"No. I have no reason to go there. I never went there when he was there, why would I go now?"

Angus shrugged. "No reason. It's just that Hector and Duncan say there's light in the house when they pass by at night."

Ian laughed. "And I suppose they think it's the *bocans*."

"No doubt. Sometimes I think they really want to see one even though they've scared themselves half to death with the idea. D'you know they've taken to carrying a lantern with them everywhere they go, even in the daylight?"

"No! I suppose they're thinking someone'll ask them to

stay for supper and they'll have to walk home in the dark."

"I guess that's their idea. Whatever, they don't want to be caught out at night without a light." Ian frowned. "D'you suppose it's just their imagination that there's light at James' place at night?"

"I don't know in the universe. I was looking after James' cows and chickens until I found a place for them, so I was up there every morning and every evening, but I was never there that late. I was always home by dusk. There were no lights there then, except for my own lantern."

"But that was months ago, wasn't it?"

"Aye, but Hector and Duncan came around just the other day with this story. I just told them to stay home at night and they wouldn't be seeing lights anywhere they shouldn't be."

Ian laughed. "As if they will. Maybe we should go up there and give them a good scare."

"Well. I thought I might go up and see if there's anything but imagination up there. D'you want to go with me? We could go this evening after supper."

"D'you mean you don't want to go alone?"

Angus laughed. "I don't believe in the *bocans*, if that's

what you're getting at. But I do believe in flesh and blood getting up to mischief, and we're not even sure that James has left the Island."

"But you're more than a match for James."

"Not if he came from behind."

Chapter 8

It was almost dark when Ian and Angus set out for James' house. Their lantern cast weird shadows into the fields and bushes around them. Somewhere close by, the squeak of a mouse caught by a hunting horned owl sounded. The silent arrival and departure of the bird made it difficult to see.

"There he is," whispered Ian. He pointed to a dark shape rising silently from the middle of the field.

"He's a beauty. He must be almost two feet long, and look at those wings." Angus stopped in the middle of the track to admire the bird in silhouette. "He's probably got his nest in Rory's woods."

"Well, that's where he's headed, anyway."

They resumed their walk.

"I'm glad we brought the lantern," said Ian. "I have no

wish to walk through Rory's woods in the dark. Rory told us once it was haunted."

Angus chuckled. "And who's it haunted by? The headless horseman?"

"Rory said it was his great-great grandmother who came to Prince Edward Island looking for her children who had settled here."

"Och, Grannie MacDonald was a respectable God-fearing woman who died and was buried on the Isle of Skye long and ever before the family immigrated. She'd never be haunting Rory's woods."

"Well, it made a good story when we were children."

Angus laughed. "It would have, too."

Rory's woods were dark. The moon had not yet risen and the stars gave no light. A light breeze from the Gulf of St. Lawrence caused the tree branches to rub and tap against each other. Night hunters rustled the undergrowth both on the ground and overhead.

"The woods is an eerie place at night," said Angus. "It almost raises a fear in me."

"I'm glad I'm not alone for I keep seeing lights that aren't there."

"Where?"

"Over there to the left. They're there when I'm looking straight ahead and when I turn my head they're gone."

"Och, it's just your imagination. Don't be saying things like that or you'll have me seeing things too."

Ian turned his head again to look to the left. "Well, I'm not so sure that it is only imagination. I looked and they're still there this time." Ian pointed to the left. See in that thickness of bush over there."

Angus' eyes followed where Ian had pointed, and squinted his eyes against his own lantern light. "I believe you're right. It's a mighty dim light whose ever it is. Let's go see who's there."

"We can't. The brook's in the way, and by the time we got there, whoever it is will be gone … If it is anyone."

"We'll just watch it then."

The light that wasn't there came and went as Angus and Ian passed in and out of shadow and darkness. It seemed to move with them, but at the same time it seemed to stay still. Sometimes there seemed to be two of them.

"I'll be glad to get to James'," muttered Ian. "I'll not come back through Rory's woods either."

"Nor I. As much as I hate to say it, maybe those two are right, there really are lights up here. Though they're likely of human origin."

Ian laughed. "D'you mean you still don't believe in the *bocans*?"

"Of course not. Any *bocans* that're around here are human *bocans*."

"Well, what do you say about that?" Ian stopped at the edge of the woods and pointed toward James' house. Its windows seemed to glow from within. Shadows came and went on the grass in front of the windows. Angus and Ian stood staring at the spectacle.

Angus began to run. "C'mon, Ian. Those are no *bocans* and I want a good look." As he ran up to the window the light grew dimmer and went out. He peered through the frame but could see nothing. The smell of tallow was heavy on the air. From the back of the house came the sound of a door being carefully closed.

"Well, that was no *bocan*," said Angus.

Ian joined him at the window. "Whoever it was has escaped by now. We'll not be able to catch him."

"Want to go inside and have a look around?"

Ian shrugged. "Might as well, but there's probably nothing there."

Their tour of the house revealed nothing but a dozen candle stubs in the parlour, stuck to various surfaces by their wax.

Angus laughed. "So much for Hector and Duncan's *bocans*."

"Yes, but they'll never believe it. Who do you think it was?"

"Tramps or gypsies likely. They've heard the story and want to keep the community stirred up just for fun."

"Some fun."

"Let's go home. There's nothing to be done here anymore tonight. We'll just have to keep a closer watch on this place."

They went for home the long way and parted at the top of Ian's hill field. Ian trudged down the track alone. *I guess Donald's gone to bed.* He closed the door and fumbled on the kitchen table for a match. His hand brushed the lantern and he frowned. *What's this doing here? It should be in the barn.*

❖

Sunday came too soon. The rooster crowed and Ian stretched hard against the aches from the previous days' work. He winced, then yawned, then rolled out of bed, his bare feet chilled almost to cramping from contact with the cold floor. The prospect of the enforced idleness of the Sabbath grated on him. *There never seems to be enough time these days,* he grumbled to himself. *I never realized before just how much work Anna accomplished in a day besides her housework. It would be easier if I could keep Donald home from school, but that would never do.* Anna had her heart set on Donald going to college. He pulled on his frosty clothing, his breath steaming the cold air of the sleeping loft. *It'll be good to get the fire started this morning.* He hurried downstairs. Donald soon followed, roused from his sleep by the banging of stove lids and the thump of wood being dropped into the wood box.

"We're invited to have dinner with Mary and Angus after church today," Ian announced. He ladled porridge into two heavy bowls. "Will you be coming too?"

"No, thank you."

"What'll you do, then?"

Donald shrugged. "Come home, I guess." He ate in

silence for a few minutes. "I thought I might sharpen the axes while I have time."

"On the Sabbath? Indeed, you won't!"

"And why not? Sunday's as good a day as any other."

"Because it's the Lord's day and we're to remember the Sabbath day and keep it holy. We're given six days to labour and do all our work, and rightly so."

"The better the day, the better the deed," said Donald. He scooped up the last of his porridge and rose from the table. "I'll start chores." He carried his bowl into the pantry.

"Well, there's *bannoch* and a bit of stew left over from last night's supper. It's on the shelf in the cellar."

I feel so helpless whenever we have dealings, thought Ian, and I still haven't said anything about the chicken. I don't have the energy to confront him with it. It'll just be the same old thing. He'll shrug and grunt and give some perfectly plausible story that we both know isn't true and we'll have the unpleasantness of another fight to deal with.

"I'll be out to help you with the rest of the chores in a moment," he said, but Donald was gone, the porch door slamming behind him.

That's another job I'll have to do. It'll soon be winter and the banking isn't done yet and the storm doors aren't on. The one to the porch needs repairing. I must pick up a new hinge at John's the next time I'm by there. He swallowed the last of his tea and rose from the table. It's been a long time since I've had occasion to go to the store. Awareness of his isolation struck him with a force he wasn't expecting. I've only seen others on business these last few months. The thought startled him, and a sense of his loneliness for the camaraderie of his male friends and relatives crept into his consciousness. I used to visit at the store every Saturday morning whether I needed anything or not. I just don't have time for frivolity and gossip anymore. He set his cup in the pantry among the stack of dirty dishes from the day before. Anna'd never have allowed her pantry to look like this. He stood for a moment looking at the week's worth of dishes, then turned his back on the mess. If I don't hurry with chores I'll be late for church. He pulled on his old sweater and hurried out the door.

It's not long before Hallowe'en, thought Ian as he trudged up the track toward the church. I wonder what mischief the boys'll be up to this year. His lips curved into a faint smile at the remembrance of some of the pranks he and his friends had carried out in their youth. He thought of the time they had dismantled old Dan Archie's wagon and reassembled it on the roof of his barn. Dan was altogether too proud of that wagon, he thought and his smile deepened. Of course, it was one of the few wagons in the district, so I guess he had a right to be proud of it. He had the horses to pull it with too, and he was never mean to lend it, though he worried about it terrible. It was his worrying and the fussiness about it that got us going. We let him fume about it overnight, then we went back and helped him take it down. His smile faded. The pranks that Donald's been pulling lately haven't been kind, and it isn't even Hallowe'en yet.

He trudged on. The cool October wind sifted through his suit coat and rattled the few remaining leaves on the birch trees. He shivered. It's soon time for an overcoat. I hope Donald shows up for church. He said he would, but he's so unreliable these days … The thought dwindled into mental silence. The white spire of the church showed against the black of the spruce trees and Ian quickened his pace.

"G'day, Ian." Several of the men standing outside greeted him.

"Where's young Donald this morning?" asked Lochie.

"He said he'll be along in a few minutes." Ian took his place among the group. "How's Rachael? I heard she had a fall the other day."

"She twisted her ankle chasing that wild calf of mine across the pasture. The doctor said it wasn't broken but she's to rest it for a few days."

"Well, now that's too bad. She'll soon be mended though, since it wasn't a break."

"Aye, and maybe she'll leave the calf-chasing to Neil from now on." Lochie's voice was stern.

"I heard that Chester's boy is back for a visit," said William. "It's good that he could come all the way from the Boston States."

"If he wanted to see his mother before she died he had to come," said Alexander.

"Is she that low, then?" asked Ian.

"Catherine said she was failing fast," replied Alexander. "She's been with her this last fortnight."

"Catherine's a good soul then, to take on that horde of

children and a sick woman besides," said William, "and her without chick nor child of her own."

"Well, she's family and the children are well-behaved," said Lochie. "Isabelle was a good mother."

"That'll leave only Catherine of that family when Isabelle goes. She'll be lonely. The two of them were awful close." Alexander's voice was sympathetic.

"Perhaps Roddy'll marry Catherine." Duncan's voice suddenly piped up from the outside of the group.

"It'd be a good solution to several problems," agreed Hector. "Roddy'd have someone to care for the little ones, and Catherine'd have a home."

"She already has a home," said Lochie, startled by Hector and Duncan's sudden appearance on the fringes of the conversation. "Anyway, Isabelle isn't dead yet, and Catherine might not want to take on eight little children at her age. She's not that young anymore."

The talk flowed over and around Ian and he was warmed by the companionship. The news of neighbours and friends suddenly thrust life forward and a sense of moving toward the future was reawakened in his heart.

"Well, I guess we should go in now, I see Mr. MacDonald

coming and he's looking at his watch," said William.

"Mr. MacDonald's a fine speaker," observed Ian as he and Angus and Mary walked home across the fields. The cool earthy smells of October were over-laden with the rich smell of roasting chicken as they entered Angus' yard. Dog bounced and barked around them as they made their way toward the house.

"Be quiet, Dog!" Angus spoke firmly and the barking ceased. "Heel!" The dog came to heel and followed them to the house.

"That's a fine obedient beast," said Ian. "You've trained him well."

"I started him when he was still a pup." Angus opened the door for Mary.

"Dinner won't be long," said Mary. "I peeled the vegetables last night, and the chicken smells about done."

"I see Donald wasn't in church." Angus settled himself on the red sandstone step by the back door. "Is he ill?"

"No, but he may be when I get ahold of him. He told me an out and out lie this morning and it isn't the first one." His anger at Donald suddenly rekindled and blazed forth into the peace of the Sabbath noon. "I don't know what I'm to do with him, I truly don't. I can't talk to him, I can't rely on him to do what he says he's going to do, I can't get a straight answer out of him on anything, and he's always got some excuse for being where he's not supposed to be." Ian's shoulders slumped as if the anger had held them up for the past several months. "I just don't know what to do."

"Perhaps he should go and work for someone else for awhile".

"Who'd have him? Besides, I can't run the farm myself."

"You used to, and with Donald at school all day, you're almost doing it all alone now."

The truth of that observation took away Ian's illusion that he was not carrying the burden of farming by himself. His shoulders slumped still further. "I'm weary now, and that was thirty years ago. I was a young man then. I don't believe I could do it now." Ian sat down on the other end of the step.

"The farm was much smaller then, too. Not nearly so many acres cleared."

Ian fell silent and thought back over the years of

backbreaking toil that had gone into clearing the land. Poppa and I worked side by side until one day Poppa sat down on a stump and said, "I cannot do this anymore," and died. After that I married Belle. She was a pretty fragile girl who wasn't able to work in the fields. She wasn't able to do much more than keep a clean house. Oh, but she was pretty and sweet, and wonderful to come home to. His heart yearned momentarily for a return to the days with Belle. Life was so easy then. At least until the baby wouldn't come, and now the two of them are lying in the same casket, the baby's bones still nestled in the curve of its mother's bones, never born.

"Come in then, dinner's on the table." Mary's voice through the open door interrupted the melancholy flow of his thoughts.

"Sit in to your usual place, Ian," said Mary. "I'll just pour the tea."

Angus pulled the extra chair from behind the stove and placed it for himself and left the stool for Mary.

Mary poured the tea and passed the cups, then settled herself comfortably on her little stool. "Angus, will you return thanks?"

They bowed their heads and Angus began a long prayer of intercession, thanks and apology. The food steamed and cooled in the serving dishes as Angus strolled on through his list of requests. Ian's stomach rumbled and his mouth watered. He swallowed hard. Angus paused to collect his thoughts and mentally review his petitions. "Oh, Lord," he began, then paused again.

"Amen," chirped Mary into the brief silence, a sparkle of mischief in her eyes. "That was a fine prayer, Angus. Pass Ian the potatoes. It's a shame Donald wouldn't join us today."

Ian spooned a generous helping of mashed potatoes onto his plate. "He was invited. He didn't even come to church as he said he would."

"Och, well, maybe something came up that he had to attend to," soothed Mary. "He's always been a responsible lad." She passed Ian the platter of chicken. "See, it roasted up well. It's so tender it's falling off the bones."

"It's a miracle then," Ian helped himself to a thigh. "The squawking and complaining that was coming out of the poor beast when Donald was butchering it, I was afraid it'd be like shoe leather."

"Well, it isn't. It roasted up just fine." Mary helped herself to the vegetables then passed them to Angus. "So, are you all snug for the winter yet?"

"Not yet," said Ian around a mouthful of potatoes and gravy. He swallowed, then said more clearly, "I was just thinking this morning that the banking isn't done and the storm windows aren't on and the storm doors need repair, and I don't know when I'm going to get to it all." He poured his steaming tea into his saucer to cool, then lifting it with his characteristic three-fingered grip, sipped noisily. "Anna'd be ashamed of the house too. I'm sorry that I've had to let it go so. There's dust in the corners and the dishes are still there since the day before yesterday. Donald won't do them and I was so tired yesterday that I just didn't do them." He looked around Mary's tidy kitchen. The curtains were bright and fresh, the floor was swept, the wood box was filled to overflowing and there wasn't a speck of dust anywhere. Anna's kitchen used to look like this, he thought.

"I've been thinking," said Mary. "There's a few of us ladies who haven't a lot to do these days. If it wouldn't offend you, we could come over some day this week and do the fall housecleaning for you."

A ray of hope leaped into Ian's eyes. "Would you? I'm afraid I've not been able to keep up with the housekeeping too."

"What do you have over there for cleaning supplies?"

Ian's face fell. "I don't know. Anna took care of all that."

"Never mind then, we'll just bring it all."

"G'day Ian, Donald." Angus set down the handles of the wheelbarrow he was pushing and began passing its contents to Mary who carried them into the house. "It's a grand day for cleaning and fixing."

"It is that." Ian turned and began to help with the unloading. "That last basket smells awfully good for lye soap."

"Well, you know Mary, she's brought enough to feed an army, besides all the other work she plans to get up to. Rachael and Eliza are coming too, and William and Lochie will be along later to help with the banking. Flora and William may be here later too. Catherine's still with her sister and can't come and Edith has to stay with Old Annie. She's ailing again so I hear. They called for the minister last evening, but she still hasn't gone."

"She may outlast all of us." Ian laughed, his heart lighter than it had been for a long time.

Voices sounded on the path and presently Rachael and Eliza came around the corner. "The other men'll be here shortly," said Rachael. "That calf's out again, and William and and Neil are trying to catch it while Lochie repairs the fence. I've never seen such an animal for getting out. Where's Mary?"

"Right here," said Mary. "My, that's a big basket, Eliza. Just bring it in and set it on the table. We'll see what has to be done. I think we should start upstairs and let the dust settle downward as we go. Where did Anna keep her laundry tub, Ian?"

"In the porch behind the door. I'll get it for you; it's very heavy to lift."

Presently the house was alive with bustle and chatter as the women set to work. "I'll just get at these dishes so we can start on the pantry when we're finished with the upstairs," said Eliza dragging the dishpan out from under the cupboard. "Flora can help me when she gets here. It won't take us long and we'll be up to help you in a few minutes." She poured hot water from the kettle into the pan and added a pinch of soap and was soon up to her wrists in her task.

Mary and Rachael climbed the steep stairs to the bedrooms. "I wonder, should we attempt to wash the mattress ticks today, or should we just refill them as they are?" Mary took down the curtains and opened the narrow window.

"They probably haven't been done since spring." Rachael pulled the covers off Ian's bed. "It looks like he hasn't had a change of sheets for some time either. We may not be able to get these clean."

"If we soak them for a bit they'll do. Lye soap is good for almost everything, and today's a good windy day for sheets." She rolled them into a bundle and tossed them down the stairs. "Let's see what condition Donald's room is in." She scurried around the corner. "Actually today would be a good day to do the ticks, we have the men here to carry them for us."

"Does Ian have lots of straw, I wonder? It's going to take a lot to refill that big tick in his room, and Donald's isn't small either."

"Oh, I think so. He had lots of oats in this year, and I think the big loft is full. He and William were talking about it just the other day. He said he thought he might sell some to make a little money."

"Isn't that just like a man, then. Never a thought for such things as mattress ticks." Mary turned up the tick on Donald's bed. "What's this?" She pushed the tick farther aside and pulled on the object tucked far toward the centre of the bed between the mattress and the ropes which supported it.

"It looks like a whiskey bottle. What would that be doing here?"

Mary frowned and pursed her lips. "I don't know, and I'll bet Ian doesn't know about it either." She thought for a moment. "Don't say a word about this to the others. I'll get Angus to take it up with Ian later." She rolled the bottle up with the sheets from Donald's bed and carried them downstairs and out to the woodshed.

The work went forward rapidly. Ian built a fire to heat water for the wash, and he and William hauled water from the well to fill the wash tub. By noon the bed ticks and sheets were flapping on the line in the sunshine and the breeze from the Strait, and the second instalment of wash was soaking in the tub.

The men were busy too. Storm windows were repaired and placed over the windows, Lochie found a hinge in his tool box and saved Ian a trip to the store for such a small errand, and soon the storm door was in place. Two of the men had brought wheelbarrows and were soon hauling loads of red clay from behind the barn and shovelling it over the foundations. It seemed a short time before Mary was calling everyone to dinner.

"You men sit in, then, and have your meal. We'll eat when you're finished. There isn't enough room for all of us at the table," said Mary. "Perhaps someone will return thanks."

Hands folded and heads bowed. "Heavenly Father," began Ian, "we have so many things to be thankful for today. The companionship and help of good neighbours and friends which continues to sustain us many days after the work is complete. The work of these fine women renews my home and my strength when I am unable." Ian's voice thickened with the strength of his affection for his friends.

He cleared his throat. "Bless every one out of the goodness of thy hands. Be with those of our friends who are ill, and with those who are attending them. Bless this food to our use and pardon our sins, in Jesus' name, amen."

"Help yourselves everyone." Mary began to bustle again. "Angus, you start the meat, William, the carrots are right in front of you, help yourself. Eliza, will you get the butter from the pantry, please? I forgot to put it on the table. Rachael, I set the cups in the warming oven, perhaps you'll pour the tea. I hope they're not too hot, I didn't have any place else to put them. I'll just go and fill the kettle again." She scurried off to the well.

"Where's Donald this morning, Ian?" asked Lochie. "I didn't see him at all."

"He was here when we came and I saw him by the barn after that," said William. "I haven't seen him since."

"I don't know where he is half the time these days," said Ian. "He never tells me where he's going, nor even if he is going. He just disappears for hours on end and reappears when it suits him."

"I've seen him around a few times," said Lochie. "I asked him where he was going and he just said he was running errands."

"Was this during the week?" asked Ian.

"The few times I've seen him it was," replied Lochie. "That's why I asked him where he was going."

"That young imp!" Anger was rough in Ian's voice. "He's supposed to be in school, and that's where I thought he was all this time. I'll have to have a word with him, for all the good it'll do."

An uncomfortable silence followed his angry words. At last Lochie said, "Aye, well, it's difficult to deal with a recalcitrant son, but I'm sure it'll come out all right in the end. I know my Neil has his days and his brothers did before him."

"It's all part of growing up," soothed Eliza.

"Pass the meat there Angus, everyone help yourselves," said Mary, "there's lots more where that came from."

"More tea?" offered Rachael.

"I'll set out the pie," said Eliza and hurried into the pantry.

"An excellent meal ladies," said William as the men trooped out of the kitchen. "I hope we left you enough."

"Oh, there's plenty left," said Mary. "I made sure of that, Ian and Donald'll have leftovers for a week." She began clearing the table of their meal. Soon the women were gathered for their own repast.

"I guess we've already returned thanks," said Eliza, "there's no need to do it again."

"I heard that Old Annie wasn't doing very well," said Rachael as she helped herself to potatoes.

"Och, Annie'll outlive us all," sniffed Eliza, "she's always having these turns. Sometimes I think it's just to keep Edith home that she does it." She passed the vegetables to Mary.

"Oh, Eliza, I don't think so," said Mary. "Annie was never mean like that, and, after all, she is a very old woman."

"No, but she's gotten sly in her old age. She was always kind of cunning and you can still see it in her eyes." Eliza picked around on the plate of meat to find a piece with a nice rim of crisp fat attached.

"I'd never have called her cunning," said Rachael. "She always struck me as being very wise, and anyway, a woman alone has to be at least a little sharp."

"Did Ian ever tell anyone what she said to him that upset him so, that time at your house, Rachael?" asked Eliza.

"Not that I know about," said Mary. "If he told anyone, it'd likely be Angus, and Angus has never said."

"It's too bad about Donald giving his father so much trouble," said Rachael to change the direction of the conversation. "He was always such a good boy when Anna was alive."

"He was far too attached to her for it to be healthy," said Flora. "I tried to tell Anna that but she just laughed and wouldn't say a word against it."

"Anna always did have a mind of her own," observed Eliza, "that's how she got into so much trouble with James, to my way of thinking. She should have just left him alone after she married Ian and especially after she had Donald. It was the cause of a lot of trouble or I miss my guess."

"Will you be needing any more wood, Aunt Mary?" Donald's voice from the doorway startled everyone.

"You can fill up the wood box if you will, dear. It'll be a great help," replied Mary.

"Well! Talk about sly! How long was he standing there?" Eliza's voice was sharp with disapproval.

"Not long. I saw him come in," said Mary. "It might be prudent to keep certain opinions to ourselves when he's about. After all, she was his mother no matter what she may have done, and he's still just a child and doesn't need to hear that sort of thing."

"Dessert for anyone?" asked Rachael. "I'll just cut another of those pies."

By suppertime Ian's house was clean and snug and returned to order. The ticks were stuffed with fresh straw and the beds were made, the curtains were starched and ironed and back in place, the clothes were washed and put away, the whole house had been swept and dusted and scrubbed, and the pantry was filled with the leftovers from their noonday meal. Ian surveyed the snugness and cleanliness of his house. It felt more like home at this moment than it had since Anna died.

"I'll have to order some glass at John's this week," said Ian, relaxing over a second cup of tea after supper. "It's wonderful to get all this done. I didn't know in the world how I was going to do it by myself."

"Well, you'd do the same if the circumstances were reversed," said Mary, "and so would Anna have done. We're all finished."

"If that's all that's to be done," said Eliza, "I think I'll go home now. I have some work of my own to do and it gets dark so early this time of year." She took off her apron and folded it into her basket, then pulled on her bonnet.

"You might as well go too, Rachael," said Mary. "I can finish up here."

"Wait and I'll walk with you, then, Eliza," said Rachael hurrying to gather her things.

"Will you help me bring in some wood, please Angus," said Mary after the others had left, ignoring the fact that Donald had already filled it to overflowing.

"Och, I can do that," protested Ian. "I'm not dead yet."

"Oh, no, just sit and enjoy your tea for a moment. It may be the last chance you have for awhile." Mary grabbed Angus by the arm and urged him out the door.

"Mary, Mary, what's the rush? The woodshed isn't going anywhere."

"No, but young Donald might be if he doesn't mend his ways." Mary pushed Angus into the woodshed. "Look what we found underneath his mattress." She pulled the bottle from its hiding place among the veterinary salves and ointments. "What do you suppose he had that for?"

"More to the point, what did he do with the contents?"

"Drank them, I suppose. I wonder if Ian knows about this?"

"I doubt he does. If he knew he'd put a stop to it." Angus sighed. "Well, I suppose I'll have to tell him. Donald'll be as mad as a hornet, but he's heading for serious trouble if this is allowed to go on."

Ian sat rocking in the shadowy kitchen after chores that evening. The sun had gone down just after supper and the kitchen was dark but Ian didn't feel like getting up to light the candle. The house smelled of beeswax and lye soap and fresh bread.

It was good of Mary to set bread for me with everything else she did too. Ian regarded the golden-domed loaves sitting on the table to cool. That will last us at least a week. His thoughts turned toward his most recent conversation with Angus.

"Well, there may be an explanation for Donald's strange behaviour. " Angus pulled the whiskey bottle from behind his back. "Mary found this under his mattress this morning. Did you know about it?"

Ian stared at the bottle as if he'd never seen one before. "No, I did not."

"D'you keep whiskey for medicinal purposes?"

"I keep a little to ward off the cold and for special occasions now and again, but that's not my bottle," said Ian. "Mine's in the cupboard in the pantry. I haven't used it since before the funeral."

"Well, Mary found this in Donald's room and she thought you should know about it."

Ian's thoughts returned to the present. Donald was as silent as ever doing chores this evening, and now he's nowhere to be found. He's as secretive as his mother was. I hardly ever knew what she was up to either. But I'll have a word with him yet about this. He got up to light the candle.

Hurrying footsteps crossed the darkening barnyard and a rap, urgent in its intensity, sounded on the porch door.

"Ian! Ian! Are you home, then?"

"Is that you, Duncan?" Ian hastened to the door.

"Come quick! Catherine's hay barracks is on fire and it's threatening her barn, and her not home to stop it."

Ian grabbed the water bucket and stuffed his feet into his shoes. "Run and tell the others! Hurry!" He blew out the candle and ran out the door and across the fields.

Catherine's barnyard was filled with sooty-faced men and boys relaying buckets of water from the well to the blazing haystack.

"Are there any animals in the barn?" Ian joined the line.

"No, Donald got them out earlier," replied William. "There was just her cow and a few chickens. Donald put the cow out to pasture and locked the chickens in the house."

"In the house?! What's the matter with the boy? There'll be an awful mess in there. He knows better than that."

"Well, they're in there," panted William, heaving another full bucket toward Ian, "and it's there they'll have to stay for now."

Ian grabbed the bucket and threw it against the barn wall where some shingles were starting to singe. The water splashed and hissed and evaporated. He passed the bucket back down the line and took the next one from William. This one was directed toward the top of the stack where it caused a momentary dampening of the blaze then turned to steam and mingled with the smoke.

"The fire's against us." Ian grunted as he heaved another bucket of water to the top of the stack.

"It was worse than this twenty minutes ago," shouted William over the crackling of the flames. "Keep working." He took the empty bucket from Ian.

After an hour the worst of the fire was over and the barn was saved. The voices of the neighbours retreated in the distance as they returned home. Only Angus, Ian and William remained. Angus stirred the remaining hay with a pitch fork. A few sparks hissed and died in the dampness.

"Was this all the hay Catherine has put up?" asked William from his seat on the sooty sandstone step of the barn.

"She has another stack behind the barn and some in the loft," said Angus.

"She'll be all right for the winter then," said Ian from the darkness of the barn doorway.

"Aye, but it's a shame to lose all that lovely hay," said William. "It might have done her for two winters."

"Or she could have sold some in the spring for a little extra money," said Ian. "She has a very small income. Just the eggs and the extra milk and the cheese and butter she makes. She barters for all the rest."

"Who discovered the fire?" asked Angus.

"It was Donald who came to get me," said William.

"It was Duncan who came and got me," said Ian. "What was Donald doing here, I wonder. He said he was going over to Neil's."

"He wasn't at Neil's," said Angus. "I was there returning Lochie's harness. I mended it for him the other day. Neil was in the kitchen doing his lessons all the while I was there."

"Drat that boy! Why doesn't he do what he says he's going to do?" Ian's displeasure put silence on the group for a few moments. "Was he here helping with the fire? I didn't see him."

"Getting in the way was more like it," said William.

"I saw him standing at the back of the barracks just before you arrived." Angus gave a final stir to the remains of the hay. "After that I don't know where he got to."

"I just don't know what to do with him anymore."

"He's still missing Anna. He's really only a boy for all his size," said Angus. "Give him a little longer and don't be too hard on him or you might lose him too. He's just at that age."

❖

"You missed all the excitement last night." Ian spoke casually in an attempt not to antagonize Donald.

"I was there," said Donald.

"I didn't see you."

"Well, I was there, and I saw you working at the head of the line."

"You didn't stay around."

"I was there long enough." Donald reached for a piece of bread.

"What did you do to your hand?"

Donald pulled his hand back and hid it in his lap. "Nothing." He clamped his lips shut.

"It looks like a burn to me."

"So I was helping with the fire last night and I got burnt."

Ian looked at his son. "I don't suppose you had anything to do with the setting of it?"

Donald smiled a secret smile. "No, but it was a lovely blaze."

Chapter 9

The next Saturday morning Ian made an effort to go to the store for an hour after chores were finished.

"G'day Ian," greeted John. "We haven't seen you for awhile. Pull up a feed sack."

Ian sat down on the nearest sack and greeted the others. The dusty dimness of the store was easy on the eyes, and the light from the big front windows was just enough to see by. Mary John kept the cobwebs at bay with her feather duster and her broom, but no one would have noticed anyway. It was the men's refuge from the cares of farming and raising families.

"That was some fire at Catherine's the other night," said Hector. "I thought for awhile we'd never get it out. I wonder how it got started."

"Spontaneous combustion, likely," said Duncan.

"Or the *bocans*," said Hector. "I wouldn't put it past the likes of them."

"Och, the *bocans*, the *bocans*, that's all you ever think of," grumbled Duncan. "More than likely it was a human *bocan* that set it, if it was set."

"Who would do the likes of that to poor Catherine?" asked Lochie. "She's never done any harm to anyone."

"The murderer, that's who," said Duncan. "We've never found him."

"Nonsense!" said William, who had just entered. "The murderer's long gone by now."

"G'day William," said John the store. "How're things out your way?"

"Oh, just the same. I see Catherine's back home."

"Yes," said Lochie, "she thought she'd better come home in case there was any more trouble. Lizzie Alexander from Flat River agreed to stay with Isabelle."

"Well, that was good of her," said Ian. "Isabelle's no kin of hers, and with all those children she'll have her hands full."

"Yes, but Lizzie's had some nursing experience in the Boston States. She worked for a rich woman down there, you know."

"So why'd she come back?" asked Duncan. "If she was making good money she should have stayed."

"The old lady died and left Lizzie a little in her will so Lizzie decided to come home."

"I heard she got down and kissed the ground when she got off the boat, she missed the Island that much," said Hector.

"If she did it at all, it was more than likely the rough passage," said Duncan. "There can be an awful swell with the cross-currents by the Bay of Fundy even on a calm day."

"Much you know about it," retorted Hector, "you've only ever been off the Island once in your life, and nearly drowned doing it."

"I know more about it than you think," said Duncan.

"About as much as I do about Catherine's fire," snapped Hector, "and that's not much."

"If you're going to come to blows, boys, take it outside," said John.

The others laughed.

"There's more to Catherine's fire than appears," said Angus. "I was just by there to see how she was and she showed me this." He held out a blackened flint and steel.

"Where'd she find that?" Ian stared hard at the items in Angus' hand.

"Out behind the barracks. That's where most of the fire was when I arrived."

"I had an old flint and steel like that in the workshop. It was my father's that he brought from Skye. I haven't used it for years."

"Well, there's no telling whose it was anymore," soothed Angus. "One flint and steel looks much like any other one."

Ian rose to his feet, his pleasure in the morning's company destroyed. "Nevertheless, I'll have another discussion with Donald."

Ian's walk homeward was filled with unhappy thoughts. Why would he do such a thing? Catherine would never deserve such a thing. Maybe he really didn't do it. Maybe someone came and took it out of my workshop. He shook his head in bewilderment. But nobody would take anything without telling me. I'd hear from them sooner or later.

Anna's Secret

His step slowed as he neared his barn. The place was silent except for the chatter of a squirrel high in the spruce tree, and the faint rustle of a raven's wings as it settled onto one of the bare branches in the apple orchard.

"Donald! Donald! Are you here, then, Donald?" There was no answer. Even the squirrel was silent.

"Drat that boy. Where has he gotten to now?" Angus looked into the emptiness of the barn. "Donald!" A rustle of hay, a sharp squeal then silence was the only response to his call. Presently the yellow barn cat appeared with the limp body of a field mouse in its mouth. "Well, Pussy, I see you've been doing your job."

The cat dropped the mouse at Ian's feet.

"Thank you, Pussy, I'll look after it." Ian picked up the mouse remains and discarded them on top of the manure pile, and began again his search for Donald.

The woodshed was empty as well, the wood for the winter neatly split and stacked to the back walls. Well, Donald, you've at least gotten the wood finished. Ian turned and retraced his steps across the barnyard and pulled open the heavy shop door. "Donald! Donald? Are you here, Donald?" His voice echoed in the emptiness.

"I guess I'd better have a look and see if Poppa's flint is still there," he muttered, stepping into the sunlit interior. He rummaged on the shelf above the workbench and found nothing. *I know I put it here. It was just this summer I saw it when I was looking for my other nail set.* His hand felt along the length of the shelf. *Well, it's not here now and I hope you haven't taken it, Donald.*

"Are you looking for something?" Donald's voice came from the doorway behind Ian. The width of Donald's shoulders blocked out most of the light, and Ian felt again that his son was a stranger to him.

"D'you know what happened to Poppa's flint and steel?" Ian frowned at the silhouette of his son. "It was up here on the shelf for years and now I can't find it."

Donald's face took on a closed look. "And you think I took it?"

"I'm just asking if you've seen it." The weariness was back in Ian's voice.

"Well, as a matter of fact, I lent it to James and Rory the other day."

Ian's face relaxed its frown. "What did those two want it for?"

"They said they were going to play settlers."

"And how did they know I had a flint, I'd like to know?"

Donald shrugged. "I told them. I didn't think they'd do any harm with it."

"Harm! Donald, where's your common sense? You don't give matches to children to play with. Och, what am I going to do with you?" Tears filled Ian's voice and he turned away.

The fall day was cold and grey, and heavy with the smell of rain. The last leaves on the birches and maples hung from their branches like tattered banners of the dead summer. It had been two days since the fire but the memory of it was still in everyone's mind. Angus strode on toward home with a steady mile-eating pace. A rustle on the path ahead of him that was neither bird nor animal caused him to interrupt his step.

"Who's there?" He moved cautiously forward.

"It's only us." James emerged from a side path followed by Rory.

"Well, g'day boys," greeted Angus. "Shouldn't you be in school this morning?"

James looked guilty. "We were sent home."

"Now why would Mr. Matheson send you home?"

"I got Rory to pass a snake to Sarah during prayers." A look of mischief sparkled in James' eyes for a moment. "It was great fun to see her jump and boy can she ever shriek!"

"Fun for you maybe," said Rory. "When she recovered she bashed me on the head with her slate."

"Where'd you find garter snakes at this time of the year?"

"We found a den of them over by the brook. They were terrible sluggish," said James.

"It's their time for sleep," said Angus. "You shouldn't be disturbing them."

"Well, I won't be disturbing them again." Rory rubbed his sore pate with a bandaged hand. "At least I won't be disturbing Sarah with them."

"I see you've hurt yourself," said Angus.

"I burnt my hand at … ," Rory stopped, his pink freckled face turning a bright red.

"I see," said Angus. "And what were you doing there?"

"Helping put the fire out," offered James giving Rory a hard nudge on his shoulder.

"I asked Rory," said Angus," and I'll ask him again, what

were you doing there?" Angus fixed the unhappy boy with his bright blue gaze.

"H-helping put the fire out?" suggested Rory.

"I was there, and I did not see you."

Rory squirmed. "We were playing settlers before the fire started."

"Playing settlers wouldn't have involved using a flint and steel, would it?" asked Angus.

James kicked Rory hard on the ankle. "Ow! Cut that out, James," exclaimed Rory.

"I asked you a question," reminded Angus, "and I expect an answer."

"Y-yes sir," faltered Rory.

"Well? Did it involve a flint and steel?"

Rory began to cry. "Only pretend at first," he sobbed. "We didn't mean for the hay to catch."

"Where'd you get the flint?" Angus was relentless.

"F-from Donald," quavered James. Tears were not far from his voice either. "He said we could use his grandfather's flint that he brought over from Scotland."

"I suppose he suggested that you play settlers in the first place?" said Angus.

"Yes sir, we were looking for something to do after chores and we saw Donald and he said we should play settlers and he got us the flint from Mr. Gillis' shop. He said we could play there at Miss Finlayson's because she wasn't home and she wouldn't mind. He said we wouldn't be disturbing anyone that way. He even showed us how to use the flint."

"I see," said Angus. "So how did the haystack catch?"

"Well, Donald said that when he used to play settlers his Poppa used to let him hollow out a little cave in the hay to pretend that it was a house and we could do the same thing. And we did, and we went to make a fire to keep warm by and just all of a sudden the haystack started to smoulder and we ran to tell Poppa but it was too late." James' tears were flowing freely by now too. "We tried to put it out but that only made it worse."

"And did you tell your Poppa?" asked Angus.

"N-no," sobbed James, "I told you, it was too late."

"What did you tell him about Rory's hand?"

"Just that he got burnt trying to help put out the fire. We both got a skelping for even being there. Momma was that savage, I thought she'd never get done with the switch."

"So was mine. It still hurts to sit." Rory rubbed his streaming nose on the sleeve of his shirt.

"And so it should," said Angus. "What you did was very wrong, and I hope you've learned your lesson from it. You could have killed someone. If Miss Finlayson had been home she might have died from trying to save her animals, or trying to put out the fire by herself. Or one of the men could have died trying to put out the blaze that you started." Angus' voice was stern. "You wouldn't want that on your conscience for the rest of your life, now would you?"

"N-no, sir," chorused the boys.

"But Donald said it would be fun to make a fire with the hay. He said it would burn beautiful," said Rory. "He said it would burn all different colours. I wanted to see the colours."

"Yes, well, now you know it's not true, and this is twice Donald's gotten you into trouble. Perhaps you'll have sense enough to stay away from him in the future."

Angus' step was heavy the rest of the way home. *Poor Ian's got his hands full. Imagine Donald putting the boys up to* something like that and giving them the means to do it. I've never seen the like.

The rain started just as Angus reached his own gate. He quickened his step to prevent getting soaked. Dog bounced and barked around him.

"Be quiet, Dog!" commanded Angus. "Go to the barn." Dog obediently turned and trotted to the open barn door and settled himself on the red sandstone step under the eaves. Angus continued toward the house. The barns'll soon need whitewashing again. The work never seems to be done around here. He opened the porch door and pulled off his shoes. "Are you home, Mary?" he called through the kitchen door.

"Aye, I'm here," said Mary from the pantry. "Are you wet then?"

"Not much," replied Angus, "I'll just sit close to the fire for awhile."

"Dinner'll be ready soon. I made a jiffy pudding for a treat. Minister MacDonald was here for you this morning. He said Annie's very low and wants to talk to you."

"Well, now, Annie's been dying off and on for years now but she's never asked for me. Perhaps she's really going to do it this time. I wonder what she wants."

"He didn't say. Perhaps he doesn't know." Mary began setting the table. "You've got your brow all creased. What's the matter?"

Angus' brow creased even further. "I ran into Rory and James in the lane. It was them that started the fire at Catherine's."

"Oh, dear-o. Their mothers'll be savage. What were they doing there and with matches too?"

"Playing settlers. Donald put them up to it and gave them the means to do it. He even suggested they start a fire with the hay because it made pretty colours."

"But hay doesn't make colours when it burns," said Mary, the cutlery forgotten in her hands. "Donald knows better than that. What in the world has gotten into him these days? His father's just heartbroken over his behaviour."

"I know," said Angus, "and I have to tell him this thing too. I seem to be always the bearer of bad news."

The rain ceased about midnight and colder winter air came on its heels.

"We'll be having snow before too long," said Angus

to Mary as he pulled on his winter coat to go and do his morning chores. "I'll have to pull the parsnips. They've had a good freeze now and I soon won't be able to get them out of the ground." He went through the porch and picked up the milk pails, surprised at the coldness of the indoor air.

He opened the door on a frozen world. Ice shimmered in the glow from the sun which had not quite come over the horizon yet. Trees bent low under the weight of the ice, their branches silvered in the early morning light. The dried grass in the fences sparkled and glowed pinkly in the rays from the rising sun. A thin shell of ice was on the puddles. Angus thought of the winter coming too soon and shivered. *I'll have to get over to see Annie this morning. I've a feeling she means it this time.* He strode across the barnyard, the wooden buckets thumping at his side.

Swinging open the barn door, he stepped into the dusty darkness and set the buckets on a shelf by the door. The white blur in the far stall moved and widened as the cow turned her face in his direction. Lighting the lantern, he hung it from its hook on the beam over his head. He opened the hatch to the manure pile outside the barn and began the task of scraping the gutters and cleaning the old straw from under the cow. The calf in the box stall watched him with curiosity then nosed around the floor for the last morsel of sweet hay from last night. Finding none she looked again at Angus and stuck her nose through the gap between the bars of her fence. "Maa … Maa." The cow turned and looked at her offspring and moved restlessly in her stall.

"It's all right bossy, she'll be fed in a minute." Angus set the manure fork in its place in the corner. He scooped a dipperful of oats from the feed bin behind the stalls and carried it to the calf. "Move over Sookie." He pushed the calf's nose out of her feed box and poured the dipperful of oats into it. "You'll have your drink in a minute."

He took down a milk bucket and pulled a milking stool over beside the cow. Balancing on the small three-legged stool he positioned the bucket between his knees, leaned his head into the cow's warm flank and began to milk. Soon the rhythm of his work brought forth a song and the cow relaxed to the sound of his mellow baritone and soft Scots Gaelic and let down her milk.

Nach lianmhor aobhar mulaid dhuinn
How often cause of sorrow comes
In our sojourn below!

Angus sang to the end of the verse, then became lost in thought.

"Indeed, bossy, we've had distress enough these last few months," said Angus into the cow's warm side, "and we've certainly needed the grace of God's blessing to see us through." He began the next verse, and continued to sing until by the end of the thirteenth verse the bucket was full of frothy milk still steaming from the cow. The cream had already started to rise as Angus set the bucket on the shelf and took down the empty one. He perched again on the milking stool and began stripping the cow. He sang the last verse over again until presently the cow was dry.

"Well, that appears to be it, Bossy." Angus lifted the bucket over the edge of the box stall and filled the calf's bucket, saving a little for the cats' dish. "I wonder where Pussy was this morning?" he said to the calf. "She's usually right here for her sup of milk. She's probably out teaching her little ones to hunt."

He hoisted the two buckets and carried them to the porch and set them to cool. Mary'll have some fine butter out of that pail. He stopped for a moment to watch the cream thicken and float on the top. Maybe there'll be a little cream for breakfast. His stomach rumbled, reminding him that he hadn't eaten yet. His wish for fresh cream was satisfied as Mary dipped a small pitcherful from the top of the bucket and brought it to the table. Ian poured a generous serving over his oatmeal and began to eat, savouring the sweet thickness of it all.

"I'll just pull those parsnips before I go over to Annie's. " He blew noisily on his tea. "I'll feed the hens too, so you needn't go out in the cold."

"Well, now, that'll be a blessing. My knees are hurting this morning. It must be the change in the weather. Have you had enough to eat? There's the end of the loaf yet. I set bread this morning but it's still just rising. It'll be ready by dinnertime." Mary got up to slice the end of the loaf for Angus. "D'you think you'll be home by then?"

"Maybe, maybe not," said Angus. "It depends on how serious Annie is and whether she's clear enough to talk this morning." He applied butter and molasses liberally to the heel of the loaf, and by careful slurping and tucking managed to get the stickiness of his breakfast past his moustache. He mopped at the residue of molasses and swallowed the last of his tea, then rose and shrugged into his coat. "I'll l be back as soon as I can." He wrapped a scarf around his neck.

The sun was beginning to melt the ice off the trees, and underfoot the path was still greasy with mud. Angus walked on the grassy verge and sometimes had to hop from tuft to tuft of grass.

Mr. MacDonald leaned on Edith's gate. The signs of weariness and a sleepless night were on his face. He stirred as Angus approached. Angus opened the gate for him.

"G'day to you, Mr. MacDonald. How's Annie?"

"Still with us, but not for long. She's been restless most of the night, asking for you. I'm just on my way home for some sleep. I sat with her all night."

"She's sensible, then?"

"She seems to be, but she's awful anxious to talk to you."

"I'd better go in then, and see what she wants." Angus closed the gate and turned down the lane.

He entered the porch and knocked on the kitchen door. "'Morning Edith, how's Annie?"

"Oh, Angus, it's so good of you to come," said Edith. "She's been asking for you all night. I've just now sat down when Mr. MacDonald left. The poor man has been here since midnight."

"I saw him. He looked worn out. I'll just see Annie, and then I'll send my Mary over to help you." His eyes took in the slight disarray of Edith's kitchen and the weariness on her face. "You'll be wanting help this morning even if it's only to spell you looking after Annie."

"Thanks, Angus, I expect I'll be needing help before this is over." Edith sighed. "Go in then, and see her. She's in the bedroom off the parlour You know where it is."

Angus went across the parlour and entered Annie's room. Her tiny body barely raised a wrinkle in the bed covers. Her thin arms lay on the outside of the blanket and her bony fingers picked nervously at the weave.

It's a good thing I came when I did, she's already picking at the sheets. I hope whatever she has to say makes sense.

"G'day Annie." He stepped toward the bed.

"Is that you at last, Angus?" Annie raised her head slightly on the pillow but did not have the strength to hold it. "Open the blinds, it's terrible dark in here and I can't see you."

Angus' heart grieved at the smallness of her voice. "The shades are open, Annie."

"Aye, well, it's worse than I thought then."

"What was it you wanted to tell me?"

"It's a long story, but I've been persuaded that I must tell it to clear the innocent." She fell silent and was quiet so long that Angus felt a pang of regret that she had passed on and not said her piece. "Annie? ... Annie?"

"Och, I'm still here. I'm just thinking how best to tell this. I was only trying to save some pain, you know."

"I know. You always were a healer."

"Tis a long story with an unhappy outcome." Annie spoke so softly that Angus could hardly hear her. He leaned closer. "It began with Anna's father ..."

Annie's voice chirped on like a cricket in the wainscoting. The sun moved around the house and gradually lightened the little room. Edith came to the door once to check on Annie, and Angus shooed her away. And still Annie talked on. Finally, just before noon she faltered.

"I'm so tired. And I'm so sorry." Her voice was barely audible.

Angus patted her hand. "You did what you thought was best, and except for the interference of others, it would have come out all right."

"Aye, well there's not much can be done about that now, is there?" Annie lay quietly for a few minutes, her bony hands no longer plucking at the sheets. "Well, I must be off," she whispered. "Why, here's Anna come for me. And doesn't she look well. Tell Ian I saw her." She lapsed into a low whisper, no longer talking to Angus.

Chapter 10

"I believe she's gone." Angus stepped into the kitchen.

"Well, now, I'll just go to her then." Edith rose from her rocker.

"I'll send Mary to you, and let Mr. MacDonald know."

"Thanks, Angus, but why don't you let Mr. MacDonald have his rest. He can come by this evening."

"I'll just go by and leave word with his wife." He closed the porch door behind himself. The day had grown into a cool high brightness. The sky seemed very far away. As Angus topped the rise he could see the white sails of a freighter sliding silently toward the south. It was well down in the water. Probably a load of potatoes for the Boston States. Angus stopped for a moment to watch the ship's progress past the coast. I doubt it'll call at the Brush Wharf, it's already too far out on the Strait. He strode on down the track. Annie's the last of the original settlers, and she wasn't even really original in the true sense of the word. It's funny, in all that great long story she never once said a word about herself. I wonder what really happened in Scotland.

A trio of ravens squabbling on the track ahead took his attention. They must have found a hare. The ravens flew heavily away at his approach, one bearing the body of a small animal. That's too big to be a hare, and the wrong colour too. Angus went to inspect the carrion. It's a cat. She's been crushed. It's Pussy! Angus swallowed hard against an up rush of bile as he recognized the yellow body of his barn cat. He turned away only to see, a little distance away, the torn form of the tiny spotted kitten who had been, just yesterday morning, climbing up his trouser leg as he milked. A few feet farther on lay another kitten. He looked for the third kitten but could not find it. I suppose that's what the raven was carrying. He pushed the tiny broken bodies to the side of the track, and strode onward.

Who would do such a thing to a harmless beast? His heels struck hard against the red clay path. His approach startled the birds into silence. "This must stop!" he muttered. "Whoever is doing these evil things must be found out." His rapid stride took him past the Minister's gate before he realized he'd done so. He turned back.

He did not stop to admire the fine dark spruces that provided the backdrop to the minister's house. It sat in the curve of their boughs, its whitewashed walls in shining contrast to their darkness. They had provided shelter to the minister and his almost grown family for the last thirty years. The outbuildings protected the other side of the house from the northeast. The small apple orchard, bare now of leaves, still held an occasional apple which would fall in the winds of the first heavy winter storm from the Atlantic Ocean.

His heavy stride carried him up to the door of the house. He raised his hand to knock loudly but the memory of the minister's tired face as he left Edith's that morning caused him to restrain himself. He rapped softly and went in.

"Are you home then, Elizabeth?" he called quietly into the dimness of the porch. Elizabeth came to the kitchen door. "Oh, it's you, Angus. Come in. He's just gotten up.

How's Annie?"

"She's gone."

"Is she now? She's the last of the original settlers, then, and a lot of history went with her."

Angus nodded. "Edith said to tell Mr. MacDonald to come when he's rested. I was just going to leave word with you but since he's up, I'll have a word with him about another matter."

"G'day Angus." Mr. MacDonald was climbing down from the sleeping loft in his stockinged feet. "Annie's gone then, is she?" He sat in the rocker and pulled on his shoes. "Elizabeth, a wee *strupach* wouldn't come amiss just now. Are you hungry, Angus?"

"Aye, it's been a long time since breakfast." Angus fidgeted in his chair. "I have an important matter to discuss with you." He began reciting the list of events which had been plaguing the community since the summer. "So beginning with Anna's murder and ending with my Pussy today, we have someone evil in our midst."

Mr. MacDonald sat rocking and stroking his greying beard throughout Angus' recital. He nodded. "I believe you're right."

"I think it's time we put a stop to him. Whoever it is has taken to killing innocent animals now, how long will it be before he murders again?" A rap sounded on the porch door. Elizabeth went to open it. It was William.

"G'day William," said Mr. MacDonald. "Have a seat."

"I will, but I don't feel like it. Someone let my animals out during the night. The hens were near frozen this morning. The fox got one of them. The rest of them were all huddled next to the hay barracks. The calf was shivering next to the barn door. She had no sense to go to the barracks with the hens. It'll be fortunate indeed, if she doesn't sicken and die on us. Whoever did it closed the barn door so the poor animals could not return." William stopped for breath.

"Who would do such a thing?" asked Angus.

"Why would they do such a thing either?" asked the minister.

"I suppose the same person who killed my barn cat last night," said Angus.

"We need to find out the person and put a stop to this. We'll not be safe in our beds until we do," said William.

"I suppose, as elders of the church, we should call a

meeting," said Angus. "Although, if that person is among us, it won't do much good."

"What else can we do? We cannot call in Paddy again. He's worse than useless," said William.

"Call a meeting of the elders for tomorrow evening," said Mr. MacDonald. "You can have it here."

Angus' step was much lighter on his way home. I think I'll just stop at Ian's for a moment, he thought, turning in at Ian's gate.

"G'day, Ian," Angus called across the yard to where Ian was mending harness in the shop doorway.

"G'day, Angus." Ian looked up from his task. "It's a great day. I just thought I'd enjoy the sunshine while I worked."

"We won't be having too many days like this anymore this year." Angus joined Ian on the sandstone step. "I was just at Mr. MacDonald's. We're calling a meeting of the elders for tomorrow evening."

"Oh?" Ian looked up from his work.

"Yes, we've had more unpleasant incidents in the community and we think things have gone far enough." He related the events of the previous night. "So you see, we have to do something before this thing goes any farther."

"But what if the person is one of the elders? Won't that let him know what your plans are?"

"If he is one of us. But can you imagine William or me or John or any of the others doing such things?"

"Well, no. It would be a hard stretch." Ian chuckled. "Can you imagine the trimming some of the wives would put on their husbands if they caught them at anything?"

Angus laughed too. "I imagine Eliza'd be right handy with the rolling pin." He rose. "Well, I must get going. I was over at Edith's this morning and sat with Annie awhile. She talked all morning, then about noontime she got kind of quiet and before I knew it, she was gone."

"Ah, well, Edith'll miss her."

"Yes, but at the same time it'll be a great care lifted from her shoulders. By the way, Annie said, just before she died, that Anna had come for her and to tell you that she was looking well."

Ian dropped his work and it lay idle in his lap as he stared at Angus. "Was she now? That's good to know. Was Annie in her right mind then?"

"She was talking sense just before that, but who knows

what Annie's right mind is these days."

"Well, right or wrong, it's a great comfort to me to hear it."

"Well, it's more than just her who sees people who have gone before, waiting for them when they're about to cross over. For whatever that's worth." Angus turned to go just as Donald drifted out of the shadowy interior of the shop. "Well, g'day, Donald. Have you been hiding in there all this time?"

Donald shrugged and didn't reply.

"Speak when you're spoken to," roared Ian.

"It's all right, Ian," said Angus. "I shouldn't have said what I did." He turned and strode off across the yard.

The damp air was heavy with the smell of wood smoke that evening. The moon had not yet risen. Here and there a star flickered. But they shed no light and the darkness was dense and cold. Ian put another stick on the fire and pulled the kettle over the open hole. It'll be a cold one tonight, he thought. I wish Donald would come in. He looked out the window across the fields. Behind the woods at the top of the hill the sky was bright and flickering. It took Ian a moment to realize its significance. Another fire! Ian pulled on his shoes, closed the stove and grabbed the lantern and a bucket.

"Donald! Donald!" His voice echoed off the barn wall. "Donald get a bucket and come, James' house is ablaze." He set off at a lumbering run across the fields. At the fork in the track he met Angus and William also running. "How long has it been burning?" he asked, his breath coming in gasps.

"I don't know." Angus was breathing just as hard. "Hector and Duncan came to get William and me. I sent them after Lochie and Alexander and a few of the others."

"That's all the near neighbours, then," said William. "It'll be too late for anyone else to get here."

They arrived at James' house just as the roof caved in, the sparks from its collapse briefly starring the blackness of the sky.

"Ah, well, we're already too late," said Ian coming to a halt at the periphery of the group of men who had gotten there before them. "My father helped build that house."

"As did mine," said William. "Was any of the furniture saved?"

"Not a thing," said Donald, joining his father from out of the darkness.

"Well, you finally got here, did you?" said Ian.

"He's been here all along," said John. "He's been helping draw water."

"Have you now?" said Ian and wished again for a more welcoming tone. "Good for you, but why didn't you come and get me?"

"There was no time." Donald stood staring into the blaze, a faint smile raising the edges of his struggling moustache. "I figured you'd see it soon enough anyway." He continued to stare into the fire. A wall collapsed inward in a great burst of flame and smoke. Donald's smile widened. "It's a lovely blaze, isn't it," he murmured.

The men stayed by the burning house until there was little danger of it spreading to the other buildings. It was almost morning before the blaze had reduced itself to a flicker here and there among the ashes. William drew buckets of water from the well until his arms ached and passed them down the line of men to Angus and Ian who poured them over the remains until only the ashes and a few blackened beams were left. One by one the men drifted toward home.

"I guess that's all we can do here," said Angus. The soot on his face hid most of the weariness there. "We might as well go home. It's almost time for chores."

"C'mon then, Donald," said Ian. He turned and started toward home. For once Donald went with him without argument.

After chores, Angus slept for most of the day. "I'm too old for these tricks," he muttered, rolling out of bed. He yawned and stretched, his joints cracking. The pain in his muscles, stiff from the run of the evening before, reminded him once more of his advancing age. He dressed and clambered down the steep stairs to the kitchen.

"You're up then," said Mary. "I'll just put the kettle on and we'll have a bite to eat. You have that meeting this evening."

"Yes, and this is just one more complaint added to the list." He pulled his chair closer to the stove.

Mary began setting the table. "What started the fire?"

"Who knows? Maybe tramps. Maybe whoever has been staying up there at night. Perhaps it's the work of the *bocans*, just like Duncan and Hector believe."

"A *bocan* of the human variety, no doubt," said Mary. "I didn't know there were tramps staying up there."

"I knew, but I didn't want to worry you."

That evening was as dark as the previous night. Angus carried a lantern to Mr. MacDonald's to light his way. William was already there when he arrived.

"Good evening, Angus," said Mr. MacDonald. "Pull up a chair. The others should be here soon."

"Mr. MacDonald was just telling me about your cats," said William. "That's a terrible thing. At first it sounded as if it was pranks that children would play, but I think it must be a vicious child to do such a thing to animals."

"Perhaps he was a man trying to make it look like a child," suggested Angus. "It wouldn't be difficult for someone with cunning."

"But who in the community would even want to do such things?" asked Mr. MacDonald. "But it must be someone nearby, for I cannot think that someone from away would have any reason to be up to such tricks."

A knock sounded on the door and he rose to answer it.

"Good evening, Lochie. Go right in and find a seat."

"Good evening, Mr. MacDonald." Lochie unwrapped his scarf and hung it with his coat on the hook behind the stove. "Don't close the door yet, the others are right behind me."

Soon all the elders had assembled and the meeting took on a more formal aspect. Sam kept the minutes and Lochie chaired the meeting.

"We were just saying that it must be someone nearby," said William. The men murmured their agreement.

"But we all live nearby," protested Murdoch from his chair beside the stove. "I can't believe it would be one of us."

"Nor I," said William. "Besides, it would take someone with an awful cold heart to kill kittens like that."

"I agree," said Sam. "I don't know anyone who would mutilate kittens like that."

"Well, let's start at the beginning," suggested Lochie. "Everything began with Anna's murder."

"Aye, and it's been all downhill ever since." Alexander stroked his beard. "I think if we find the murderer we'll find the author of the rest of the badness around here."

"I thought it had been pretty well proven that James had

murdered Anna," said Sam. "After all, it was him who ran."

"We don't know for sure if it was him," said Angus. "The evidence certainly pointed directly at him, but as far as we can figure out, he had no motive. I think he may just have discovered her body and panicked."

"Well, whoever did it must be still around," said William. "Perhaps James didn't run away after all. Maybe he just bought a ticket to the Boston States, got off in Summerside and came back."

"Maybe he never got on the ship at all," suggested Callum. "Maybe he just pretended to."

"Perhaps it's him who's been making fairy lights on top of Ian's big hill this fall," said David. "Mattie and I were walking home from church one evening and we passed by there and saw them. As we approached they all winked out but one, and when we got there we discovered it was only the butt of a candle. We figured it was children playing pranks."

"Is that why you never mentioned it?" asked Angus.

"I never thought about it again until just now," said David. "Why? D'you think it's significant?"

"Och, anything's significant right now," said Angus.

"I'm weary to death of the whole thing. It's about all I think of these days, and I'm no wiser now than I was when it all began."

"Perhaps it was Ian himself who murdered Anna," suggested Murdoch. "It would have taken a fairly big person to do that kind of damage to her and he certainly had reason enough."

"Unreason, is more like it," said Lochie. "Who in his right mind would pick up an axe and bash someone in the head with it? Whoever did it would have had to lie in wait for her."

"And would have had to stay there for some minutes afterwards if she was arranged as neatly as you say she was, Angus," said Mr. MacDonald. "It must have been someone who cared a great deal for her to have done that."

"Aye, she was arranged neatly, all right." Angus scowled, his mind not quite with the conversation. "The hem of her dress was pulled down to her ankles and she was lying on her back with her hands folded on her chest." His face cleared. "In fact, she was made ready for the coffin."

"Have you thought of something, Angus?" asked Lochie.

Angus' face took on a closed look. "Nothing I can be sure of. It's just a suspicion that crossed my mind. I'll look into it tomorrow to see if I'm right."

"D'you think you should be doing this alone?" asked Lochie. "If the murderer is still out there he could be lying in wait for you the next time."

"I doubt that. If it's what I'm thinking, he won't be after me."

"Hector and Duncan have been going on about lights up at James' house lately," said Mr. MacDonald. "Does anyone know anything about that?"

"I do," said Angus. "Ian and I went up there the other evening after dark and found a row of candles that had just recently been put out. They were still warm and smoking when we got there."

"D'you suppose someone's living up there?" asked Callum.

"I thought so once, but now it doesn't look so much like it anymore. The candles were arranged in the shape of a cross on that oak side table that Jean was always so proud of. There were twelve of them."

"That sounds a little too ritualistic for it to have been

gypsies or tramps," said Mr. MacDonald.

"It sounds as if whoever set them up wanted us to think it was significant," said David. "Perhaps he just wants us to think it has some connection to everything else that has been going on around here."

"Well, I went back the next day to gather up the candles and they were gone, and the table was put back in its usual place."

The men were silent for a few minutes.

"I've been thinking," said William presently, "would it be worthwhile for us to patrol the community at night?"

"We may have to," replied Angus. "Though what good it'll do is beyond me. We could be at Lochie's and the quarry could be at Catherine's setting more fires."

"That's true," said Mr. MacDonald, "but wouldn't our presence have a deterrent effect on the rascal?"

"Well, there is that aspect of it." Angus closed his eyes and appeared to be thinking. Presently he opened them and said, "If we patrol in pairs and announce our presence so as not to scare the residents when we come by, it might work."

"Is our purpose just to prevent further evil or is it to catch the scoundrel?" asked William. "If we don't scare the residents we won't be scaring the perpetrator either."

"That's true," agreed Mr. MacDonald. "Otherwise, we'll just be warning him off."

"As far as that goes," said David, "all of you who have had things happening at your place while you were there have dogs. Why didn't they raise an alarm?"

"Good question," said Lochie, "my dog even barks when I come home until he sees who it is. The only ones he doesn't bark at are the children. He always seems to know them."

Angus frowned. "Come to think of it, my dog does the same thing. The children play with him on their way to school and there's not a murmur out of him. Of course, until last night, no one has been around my place at all, as far as I know."

"As far as you know," said Callum. "The rascal could have been around our houses a dozen times and we'd never know it if the dogs didn't bark."

"All the more reason for patrols," said Sam.

"So is everyone in favour of patrols?" asked Lochie.

"It seems to be our only recourse," said William. The others nodded.

"We'll do it then. We'll divide up in pairs and each take a different night. Can we report to you, Angus, if we find anything out of place?"

"Aye, and I'll take the first watch with William. I've slept all day so we can start tonight, if it's alright with you, William." They rose to leave.

"Well, it's been a worthwhile meeting." Mr. MacDonald saw them to the door.

"We've accomplished a lot," said Lochie, shrugging into his coat. "Rachael will be relieved that we've come up with a plan."

"I expect all the women will be glad for that," replied the minister. "I know my Elizabeth will be. I'm gone so much in the evening and she has to stay by herself. It's been very hard on her."

"Eliza's been minding it too." William wrapped his scarf around his neck and tucked the loose ends into his coat. "She stayed home from church last Sunday evening and when I came home I found the door bolted. She'd fallen asleep in the rocker and didn't hear me knock. I thought for awhile I'd have to sleep in the barn." He stepped out into the darkness of the night.

William and Angus set out down the lane. The night air was still and crisp and smelled of frost. Dried grass crunched under their feet as they made their way down the track. The rustle of animals hunting in the bushes startled them more than once and they were grateful for Angus' lantern.

"What were you thinking of during the meeting, Angus?"

"Oh, I was just putting two and two together and coming up with five," said Angus. "It was something that Mr. MacDonald said made me think of young James and Rory and the prank they were up to with Catherine's cats. I don't know why I associated Anna's murder with those two and their tricks but it made clear sense at the time."

"You don't think it was them, do you? They're just two little boys. They wouldn't have the height nor the strength to wield an axe and do that kind of damage with it."

"No, of course I don't think it was them. I don't know why I thought of them and Anna together. Probably only because they were out at night and up to no good." He fell silent and they trudged onward.

"I expect you'll want to tell Eliza what we're up to, and

I have to see Mary before we start out. I'll see you in an hour at my house. Here, take my lantern to light your way."

The patrols went on for several weeks with nothing new to add except reports from Duncan and Hector about fairy lights and *bocans*.

"It seems as if the author of these events knows where we are and who is going to be patrolling every night," said Angus. "The only time there's any mischief is if Hector and Duncan are about."

"D'you suppose they're behind the mischief?" asked William. "I can't imagine them being clever enough to hide something like this for this long. The two of them can't keep a secret for more than five minutes to save their souls."

"No, I don't think it's them. I think it's someone who knows them well enough to be pulling the pranks on them and making them look like worse clowns than they already are."

"It would have to be someone who knew who was patrolling on any particular night."

"True. So we'll just have to be more clever. Supposing we patrol some night in place of them? Or go with them and not tell anyone?"

❖

"We'll go with you boys tonight," said Angus coming up behind Hector and Duncan on the dark track.

"The *bocans*," shrieked Hector. He grabbed Duncan's arm and began to run.

Angus started after them.

"Och, let them go, Angus," said William. "They'll run out of wind soon enough and we'll catch up to them without wearing ourselves out."

The two men strode on in silence and came upon Hector and Duncan on the other side of Lochie's pasture stream. Duncan was wet to his knees.

"You *gommach*! Why'd you have to go and trip me just as I was crossing the stream?"

"It wasn't me. It was the *bocans*."

"It was your big clumsy foot that got in my way. Now I'm soaked and I'll have to stay that way for the rest of the night."

"It's nice to see you boys getting along so well," said Angus from the other side of the brook.

"It's them again," whispered Hector. "I can see the fire

in their eyes."

"Well, they're over there and we're over here," said Duncan, "and I'm too tired to run any farther."

"That's right. Yoohoo, Mr. *Bocan*, you cannot catch us tonight. You're on that side and we're over here."

"Will you two stop it," said Angus. "It's only William and me. We've come to keep you company."

"Oh, and was that you on the track by Lochie's too?"

Angus and William looked at one another.

"No, we just came from Angus'." William kept a straight face with difficulty.

"See, I told you it was the *bocans*," said Hector. "They were even calling our names the other night."

"They did?" asked Angus.

"Oh, they did, they did," said Duncan. "And laughed when they were doing it."

"We're right glad you decided to come with us," said Hector. "I haven't much courage left for this job."

"Well, we're here, so let's get on with it. The night's long and from the look of the stars it's apt to be a cold one." William balanced across the brook on the stepping stones. Angus followed. Together they strode up the pasture on the other side.

"C'mon, Duncan, I don't want to be here by myself with spirits about." Hector scrambled after William and Angus.

"Where was it exactly that you saw the fairy lights?" asked Angus.

"On top of Ian's hill field, right where we found Anna," said Duncan. "There were about twelve of them, all bobbing and flitting about."

"You're not going back there, are you?" asked Hector. "They're liable to be waiting for us."

"How will they know to be waiting for you?" asked William.

"Well, we go the same way every night. It's the safest route and we can always get across running water if we need to," said Hector.

Angus grunted. "It's no wonder they know when to be waiting for you if you're in the same place every night at the same time and follow the same route. I don't suppose you had the courage to go and see what was making the lights either, did you?"

"I wouldn't go up on that hill in broad daylight now," replied Hector. "Besides the lights went out as soon as we saw them."

"You mean as soon as you hollered," said Duncan. "You almost ran over me in your haste to get away."

"Did they go out all at once?"

"No, said Duncan, "they went out one at a time."

"As if someone was up there putting them out," said Angus. "What time did you usually arrive there?"

"In a few minutes," said Duncan.

"Well, if we hurry, we may be able to catch the scoundrel setting up his little tricks. Let's go."

Angus and William hurried across the pasture and over the fence. Hector and Duncan scuttled along behind them.

"D'you suppose we should let Hector and Duncan go up the hill alone?" asked William. "That way we may be able to see who's behind it all."

"D'you suppose we can persuade them to go alone?"

William laughed. "We can only try."

They trudged on in silence. Angus half listened to the argument going on behind him. It's no wonder they could never catch the scoundrel. He could hear them coming a mile away. "Hush, you two. We're getting close."

For once Hector and Duncan did as they were told.

William and Angus stopped at the edge of Rory's woods and looked out on Ian's hill field. "Well, I guess those two weren't imagining things," whispered William. "There's six lights in a circle out there."

"Of course, we weren't imagining things," said Hector. "I told you we saw fairy lights and we did, and it was right in the spot where we found Anna, too."

"Be quiet," said Angus. He watched the lights in silence for a few moments. Presently he said: "There's someone out there. I can just see him when he moves."

"Well, he must be human, for you cannot see the *bocans*," said Hector.

"Will you two go out there as if you were on patrol, then?" asked Angus. "We'll stay here and watch what he does and where he goes."

"If you promise not to run away," said Duncan. "If the murderer was big enough to fell a strapping woman like Anna, he's big enough to finish one of us."

"We'll be right here. While you're at it, see if you can drive him this way when he leaves," said William.

"You're not going to try and catch him, are you?" asked Hector.

"Of course we are," said Angus. "There's not much point in just scaring him away."

"Well, rather you than me, he's pretty big," said Duncan. "C'mon Hector."

"If you're sure it isn't just a big *bocan*," said Hector. "They can change their shapes whenever they want, you know."

"Aye, they're that devious," said Angus. "Now, will you two get going, and don't give us away." He gave Hector and Duncan a slight push.

Hector and Duncan soon became as dark a shadow as the "*bocan*" on the hill. As they quarrelled their way across the slope, one by one the lights blinked out and the odour of hot tallow and smoke drifted on the night air. They stopped and stood staring. Somewhere close behind them an owl hooted. They shrieked and began to run. Laughter followed them as the dark shape stood in the shelter of a tree and watched them heading for the nearest brook.

"Well, that's no *bocan*," whispered Angus.

"I've never heard tell that they laughed," said William.

The dark shape moved out of the shelter of its tree. It crouched low and moved quickly across the brow of the hill.

"What's he doing?" whispered William.

"Probably picking up his candles."

The figure straightened and began moving toward Rory's woods.

"Quiet! He's coming." Angus and William crouched low behind their bushes. The figure drew near. "Now!" cried Angus. He rose and stepped in front of the dark shape. William stepped in behind it. The dark figure stopped and stood still for a moment, then ran straight at Angus, pushing him roughly down.

Angus gasped as the air was knocked out of his lungs. "Drat it! He's getting away!" The figure was soon lost in the tangle of undergrowth.

William assisted Angus to his feet. "Well, at least we know now that he's real and not just someone's imagination. You're not hurt, are you?"

"No, just angry. If I had been a younger man I could have caught him." Angus rubbed his stomach.

"No one could sustain a blow to the guts like that fellow delivered any better than you did. Are you sure you're all right?"

"I'm fine " Angus took a deep breath and squared his

shoulders. "I suppose we should try to follow him."

William shrugged. "Not much use to now. He's well away. Did you get a look at him, at all?"

"Not at his face, it was too dark. Besides, he had a hat or something on, though he's about my height and build. I got a sense of a younger man. He smelled as if he'd been drinking."

"Aye, I got a whiff of that too, so it must be someone who buys liquor. I wonder if John can give us a clue."

"Probably not. Anyone who keeps liquor buys from him."

"Well, I guess we should at least try to find Hector and Duncan."

Angus laughed, then coughed. "They're likely halfway to Charlottetown by now."

William laughed too. "That was a great imitation of an owl you did."

Chapter 11

"I fed the hens for you, Mary." Angus hung his coat behind the stove and sat in the rocker to pull off his shoes.

"Then they're well fed this morning for I was just out myself not too long ago. I heard you singing." Mary gave the porridge a stir and then returned to setting the table.

"Bossy milks better when I sing to her and it helps me think."

"And what were you thinking about?"

"What do I ever think about these days but Anna and Ian and Donald and the murder?"

"Indeed, I find my mind occupied with the matter too. How was your patrol last night? I was so tired I didn't even hear you come in."

"I was back early. There really are fairy lights in Ian's hill field, but it's not the fairies who are lighting them."

"Did you see someone then?"

"Aye, and felt him too. William and I almost caught him, but he poked me a good one in the stomach and got away."

"Where were Hector and Duncan?"

"Och, those two. They were well on their way to Charlottetown by that time."

"Well, they're not much use, are they. And were you hurt?"

"I had my wind knocked out for a moment and he shoved me to the ground. But I wasn't hurt."

"And now the rascal knows you're on the lookout for him and he'll be cannier than ever."

"He's at a disadvantage now though. He left this behind." Angus rummaged in his pocket and pulled something out. "Have you ever seen the like of this?" He opened his hand to reveal a wooden button almost an inch in diameter. Its centre was carved into the design of a Celtic cross. The carving was rough but showed a certain skill on the part of the carver.

"What good is an old wooden button?" Mary picked it up and turned it over in her hand. "It looks like a set that Annie gave Anna when she said that Anna had learned all that she could teach her about healing. Annie had an identical set on her own cloak. I believe Willie MacRae from over in Wood Islands carved them for her."

"D'you know what Anna did with hers?"

"I suppose she sewed them on something. Maybe she saved them. I really have no idea." Mary handed the button back to Angus. "You might ask Ian the next time you see him."

Angus stood looking at his woodpile and thinking. There's about four cords here. That'll keep us until spring if I get it all split. I still have time before supper to chop a few more pieces. He reached for a length of log and balanced it on its end on the chopping block. This one's a big one. He raised the axe over his head and brought it down surely on the end of the birch log. It split cleanly from end to end. The thunk of the axe and the tearing sound of its splitting echoed off the barn walls. That should make two more each. He balanced half the stick on end and held it with his left hand while tapping the blade of the axe into the top end. When the wood was secured he raised stick and axe together and brought them down on the chopping block at once. The wood again split cleanly in half.

Angus soon fell into the rhythm of his work and his thoughts began to wander. A stubborn knot brought his axe to a bone-shuddering halt. This must have been what it was like for Anna's murderer, he thought, then shivered. I shouldn't be thinking like this. It's morbid. He wrestled the axe out of the block of wood and took aim again. The wood parted with a satisfying crack.

I wonder who that was last night. It was someone who drinks, for I could smell the whiskey off his breath when he pushed me. It was someone strong for I could feel him through his coat. It was someone clever enough to take note of when Hector and Duncan were patrolling and use their superstitions to his advantage. So it has to be someone who knows them. Who else besides the elders knew when we would be patrolling? I mentioned once to Ian that Hector and Duncan would be going that night but we took different shifts. Angus fished in his pocket and drew out the button. He stood studying it for a moment. If this is

Anna's, who was wearing her cloak? Someone strong, who smelled of whiskey, who knew when Hector and Duncan would be patrolling. Ian? No, it would never be him up to such tricks. Besides, whoever it was, was too tall for it to be Ian, and anyway, Ian doesn't drink to excess. Angus blinked and frowned as the memory of his conversation with Mary in Ian's woodshed came to mind. Donald. Other bits of conversations and odd things he had seen but not particularly noted came flashing back. Angus set the axe down and went toward the house.

"Mary, I think I have discovered the perpetrator of the pranks." Angus paced the width of the small kitchen. "I wish I hadn't, but there it is in plain view. I should have seen it before. I don't know why I didn't, but I guess I didn't want to."

Mary stirred the stew sending small droplets over the edge of the pot to hiss and die on the stove top. "And who might that be?"

"You'll not believe it."

Mary set the cover of the stew pot back on with a clang and bustled over to the pantry. "Well, I won't be able to believe or disbelieve until you tell me." She gathered the cutlery and began setting the table.

"I think it was Donald."

The cutlery fell from Mary's hand with a little crash. "So it is true. I've had my suspicions for some time now. Oh, dear-o!"

Angus brought together the facts as he saw them and recited them to Mary. "So, I'm very much afraid that it is Donald."

Mary sat down on her little stool. "How'll you ever tell Ian? You will have to tell him."

Angus nodded. "I'll go over this evening."

"Oh, dear, the poor man. And he's had so much to bear lately, and now this too." Mary rocked herself back and forth. "How will he ever bear this?"

Angus went to Ian in the early darkness of the November evening. Donald was not around. There was an uneasy silence about the farm yard. In the darkness the cow bawled from the barn. Angus rapped on the door. There was no answer. He rapped again, then stepped aside to peer in at the window. He could see Ian sitting slumped over in the rocker. He pushed open the porch door and hurried into the kitchen.

Ian raised his head and stared at his cousin and best friend. "It was him," he whispered.

Angus drew a deep breath. "Where is he?"

"Gone," said Ian. "He took all the money for his education and left. We had a terrible fight. God help me, I almost accused him of murdering his mother."

Angus' eyes narrowed slightly. "Indeed, you must have been angry to accuse your son of such a thing."

"It was bad enough what I did accuse him of. The worst of it was, he admitted to most of it." Ian groaned and rubbed his eyes with the heel of his hand. "He said he started the fires at both Catherine's and at James'."

"I know, I figured it out. But why would he do such a thing?"

"He said he liked starting fires. He said it made him feel good to watch them burn and get bigger and consume all the evil in the world. He was like a man possessed."

"I suppose he implicated James and Little Rory to take the suspicion away from himself."

"He didn't say, but I wouldn't put it past him. I never knew my son could be so cunning." The rocker squeaked as Ian leaned back in it and closed his eyes. "I guess I never knew my son."

Angus searched in the pantry for Ian's bottle of whiskey. There was one small glassful left in it. He poured the whiskey into a cup sitting on the sideboard with the residue of tea leaves in it from some past meal. The tea leaves floated and the scum of cream that had dried on the bottom melted, turning the whiskey opaque. He brought the cup to Ian.

"Drink this, you probably need it." He thrust the cup into Ian's unsteady hands. "When did you find out?"

Ian stirred in the rocker. "This afternoon right before supper. I had just finished lighting the candle. We were into another of those pointless roundabout arguments we've been having since his mother died, and he let it slip. How he's carried the guilt of his behaviour all this time, I don't know." Ian sipped at the whiskey, then downed it in one gulp. "I've been sitting here ever since trying to make sense of it."

"Have you eaten?"

Ian looked puzzled for a moment. "No, I guess I haven't. The poor cow hasn't been milked either."

"She can wait a few more minutes. I'll just make you a

cup of tea and a biscuit." Angus rummaged in the wood box for the two remaining sticks of wood, then poked about in the stove for a coal to start a new fire with. In a few minutes the fire was blazing and the kettle was beginning to groan and sing. The kitchen seemed cheerier for the warmth.

Angus searched the tiny pantry for a clean plate and cup. There were none. I'll just have to rinse one of these, he thought. He looked around for the water dipper. He managed to set a place at the table for Ian, and poured tea for him. "All I could find was the end of the 'bonnick' and a little cheese and molasses."

"I guess that's all that's here. I was going to make a 'bonnick' this evening but …" Ian's voice trailed away. "I haven't had time to do much cooking this week."

"You'll come home with me this evening. We have lots of room and Mary won't mind a bit. We'll do chores before we go. Can you tell me what happened?"

"It was dreadful." Ian laid down his knife and stared at the wall. "We got into it again when I asked for an explanation about his presence at James' fire the other evening. It seemed a strange thing that he could have gotten there before I did when he'd gone up to bed an hour before.

I know he hated James, but I never thought he'd go so far." Ian fell silent.

"Go on," prompted Angus after a moment.

"Well, one thing led to another and I accused him of setting the fire. I didn't mean to because I didn't really think he had, but this queer look came over his face and I knew. So I demanded an answer, and as usual he wouldn't give me one. He just said, 'Well, you left all that lovely straw in his parlour just right for burning. Are you sure it wasn't you?' The very idea! I almost hit him."

"But you were going to burn the house down in a fit of rage one time, too. You told me so yourself."

"Aye, but that was only momentary. Donald didn't even have that excuse. He burned it just for the pleasure of doing it. He told me himself."

"A queer sort of pleasure."

"Indeed it was. I asked him what the pleasure had been, and he said, 'all that lovely bright fire and smoke, and the excitement of watching sin going up in flames.' It was as if he was in a trance."

"I suppose he meant the sin of Anna and James."

"I expect so. Though I still cannot believe that Anna

sinned. It just wasn't like her. I know she saw a lot of James but I don't believe for a minute that they had anything to do with each other that way."

"She didn't. James was her brother. Edith had an indiscretion while she was still a girl, and James was the result. Edith was very young and didn't want the baby, and of course neither did her mother because of the scandal. Annie attended the birth and agreed to take the baby to Charlottetown to the orphanage. But before Annie could arrange the transfer, Jean, who was married to James Ban, gave birth to a still-born infant, and not her first one. You remember the rumours about her miscarriages and still births. So Annie gave Edith's baby to Jean, and Jean and James Ban agreed that they would bring him up and say nothing to anyone. They named him James after his adopted father. Annie told me this the morning she died."

"And Sandy married Edith, and they had Anna." Ian shook his head. "But how did Anna know that James was her brother? Did her mother tell her?"

"No. Baby James took after his mother's people and was always small, and Old Annie and Jean passed him off as premature to account for him being so small. But I think

Edith suspected."

"I'm surprised no one else guessed," said Ian.

"Well, James looked so much like Jean's side of the family there was no real way of telling, and any speculation died when they saw how proud of his son James Ban was. I suppose they thought that he would know and be ashamed. But of course he didn't want anyone to know, so he didn't act ashamed. So when Anna started seeing James as a possible suitor, it scared Jean. She was afraid of having idiot grandchildren, never mind that she'd be committing more sin if she allowed it to continue, thinking as she did."

"I wonder if Anna knew the reason that she and James couldn't go on seeing one another?"

"She did. Annie told her before you and she were married. Anna was reluctant to marry you because she felt she was too young and unsettled and thought she was still in love with James. So Annie set her straight. Why else would she continue seeing him against her father's wishes, and against you, and create talk about herself into the bargain? She knew, and Annie swore her to secrecy."

"And Anna's word was always her bond," interrupted Ian. "I always had a hard time extracting a promise from her, but once she gave her word she never broke it. So Anna just kept quiet and let everyone think the worst of her. How like her!" Ian's face crept into a smile at the memory of Anna's kindnesses to anyone who came within her circle. "I just knew she couldn't have done those things that everyone was talking about." The smile faded. "And our son tried to burn up the evil."

"Why'd he do it?"

Ian stopped rocking. "He said he did it for me. The boys at school said she was a whore, and it worked on him. He thought he was doing me a favour. I never realized how deeply he felt about me, he always seemed so much her son. A favour, no less!"

The two men sat silently for a few minutes. Then Ian spoke: "Maybe that was what Old Annie meant."

"When she whispered to you?"

"Yes. She said, 'From Anna's blood flows blood, and more is yet to come.' It scared me!"

"You think she meant that Donald did his mischief because of Anna's murder?"

"Yes, don't you?"

"I suppose so." Angus stared at Ian. Annie was right, but

Ian doesn't understand. It wasn't just the pranks Donald was responsible for. He hasn't figured it out yet, and Donald has run off. What am I to do? The answer came in Mary's tones. "Do nothing. It will do no good for Anna, and certainly none for Ian, and Donald can fend for himself." The voice came so clearly that Angus startled and looked around for Mary. She was not there.

A chunk of wood fell in the stove, and the candle sputtered, then flared again. In the barn the cow bellowed. Ian stirred in his chair.

"I guess I'd better go and see to chores," he said.

Angus looked at him keenly. "You're feeling better, then?"

"A little." Ian was silent for a few moments. "Donald'll have to live with what he's done for the rest of his life. How I'll live with it either, I don't know. I have been sore afflicted these many months, not unlike Job."

"Ah, yes, but 'the Lord blessed the latter end of Job more than his beginning,'" said Angus.

"Perhaps it will be so with me," said Ian rising and putting on his coat.

In the barn the cow's distress crescendoed. She turned

her head and tried to move away from the thing hanging from the rafters by her side. It gently tapped her on her soft warm flank as it swung in the cold autumn wind sifting through the barn.

"Good night, Edith. Good night, Annie." Anna closed the porch door behind herself and turned toward home. The July night was warm. A little breeze lifted a loose strand of Anna's auburn hair as she walked. She thought about her latest conversation with Annie.

Annie has kept such secrets all these years. In my own case too. I'm glad she told me about it when I was so young and thought I was in love with James. It's no wonder that Poppa was so determined that I would marry Ian. I'm glad he did. I was beginning to realize what a dreamer James was and what poor husband material, but no one ever knew that.

Her thoughts wandered on. That Momma never caught on what Old Annie had done with her first child is a wonder. She was always so smart with other people's affairs. Maybe she guessed. Maybe that's why she was always so short-tempered when Jean was around. I know she was hard put not to smile when Poppa told her that Jean had died having James' sister. I was only six. Poppa came in from the store that Saturday and said:

"Well, you'll be relieved to know that Jean won't be bothering you with her presence anymore."

"And why not?" Momma just crashed the plate on the table. It almost broke. I kept very still. Momma could be awful savage when she was in the plate-crashing mood.

"She's dead, and the baby too," said Poppa. "Now you can be happy."

Momma's face was a picture. It looked like she was trying to keep from smiling. A strange kind of choking sound came out of her too. I thought at first she was crying, but when I saw her face I thought maybe it was a laugh instead. She composed herself quickly and said: "Dinner's ready. When's the funeral?"

"Saturday," said Poppa, and didn't stay for dinner.

We all went to the funeral. It's the first one I remember being at. Everyone was there. The church was full, even the balcony. Jean was well-liked for miles around. There weren't nearly that many at Momma's funeral. But then, she was a much harder woman than Jean. We all filed past the coffin to pay our respects. Jean was so white and still, not at all like herself. Her mouth was a little agape and her skin looked yellow and waxy. She held the baby in her left arm. Its face looked all squashed. I got very cold and lonely when I looked at them. It took me until mid-week to get warm again. After the burial Poppa took us home and then went to the barn and got roaring drunk. I never saw him so full before nor since. After that everyone at our house was changed. They were so cold I thought they hated each other. And then I thought they started hating me. I was so miserable. I thought no one would ever love me again. Only James had any time for me. He was the only one I could confide in and I spent every minute I could with him. He was my only friend. Poppa didn't like it, but I never knew why. The older I got, the more adamant he got. He even turned me over to the elders once. Anna chuckled to herself. They didn't know what to do with me any more than Poppa did, and I kept on seeing James anyway.

Some people think I was forced into marrying Ian and that he's just an old man. I always looked up to Ian even when I was little. I never thought I'd be married to him. When Poppa told me I was to marry him it was no effort to promise not to see James again. I saw James once more after that until he came back to tend his father's farm. I just wanted to tell him my news and Poppa caught me and had a private talk with him. James left the Island the next day and didn't come back for years until his father sickened and then died. He didn't even wait for the wedding.

Anna's thoughts turned back to Ian. *I am a very lucky woman to have such a husband as Ian. I wish I could tell him that, but it would just embarrass him.* She stood at the top of the rise and looked down at her home and its barns and sheds. *It looks so secure. And there's Ian going into the house. He must have just finished chores.* Presently a light appeared in the window. *He's put the candle in the window for me. He's always so thoughtful. I suppose I should have told him where I was going, but he never seems to mind and he had already gone out to milk when I was ready to leave.* Her thoughts meandered on to her conversation with Annie so many years ago. *It was a strange story. I wonder if James knows it. Probably not, but I cannot tell him, I promised Annie. Besides, I only ever see him in church.* Anna stretched and took a deep breath. *The air is so fresh at this time of the day. I love these solitary walks, I'm glad*

Ian doesn't mind when I traipse off alone for the afternoon. That's how I found those good strawberries. I must take Edith a jar of the jam I made. Annie's getting so forgetful these days, poor Edith has her hands full just to look after her. Anna sighed. Forgetful or not, I'll miss Annie when she goes, and if tonight is any indication she's not going to be with us much longer.

The great orange globe of the moon slipped over the horizon and slowly paled to the whiteness of new cheese as it rose. Its light threw shadows in strange places calling Anna's attention to her isolation so near to home. The sound of footsteps on the path ahead of her caught her attention and drew her completely out of her revery.

Why it's Donald come to meet me. He's grown into such a fine young man, so like Ian in his stature. She smiled to herself. Donald thinks such deep thoughts, he'll make a fine scholar. It's too bad I couldn't have had another. Ian would have been so proud. She waited at the top of the track for Donald to join her. He was carrying an axe.

"Hello, my love. You've come to meet me."

"Indeed I have, mother."

NOVELS BY MARGARET A. WESTLIE

SELKIRK STORIES

Mattie's Story

Anna's Secret

An Irregular Marriage

HAUNTED PEI

Shades of Molly

Molly and Company

Ghost Baby

Join the community!
Scan the code below or go to
www.margaretwestlie.com

Made in the USA
Charleston, SC
18 February 2014